MAJOR LEAGUE
Love

A MAJOR LEAGUE
Love

DOMENIC MELILLO

Phase Publishing, LLC
Seattle, WA

Text and cover art copyright © 2021 by
Domenic Melillo

Cover art by Melissa Williams Design

Phase Publishing, LLC first paperback edition
February 2021

ISBN 978-1-952103-19-3
Library of Congress Control Number 2021901029
Cataloging-in-Publication Data on file.

DEDICATIONS

To Susan:

We wondered "what if?", and I imagined.
We thought "if only", and I dreamed.
We told each other grand tales, and I
remembered.

You said make it so, and I did.
There are many ways to make a dream real.
This is for you.

Love, Domenic

CHAPTER ONE

Spring 1980

"I don't understand," she said, "Are you breaking up with me? Is that what this is? How can you do this to me, to us, after all we've been through together? I won't let you do it."

"Look, Maria," he responded, lowering his eyes and rubbing his forehead, "things have not been good between us for a very long time, and you know it. I have not been happy. I haven't been myself. We're young and love shouldn't be this hard. It definitely should not take this much work. It shouldn't be such a struggle."

Reaching out with her hand she gently lifted his chin so that she was looking directly into his eyes. "How many relationships have you been in, Luca?" she asked. "Two or three? How long did those last? Two, maybe three months at most? You have no idea what love is. You enjoy the early romantic part. The unlimited possibilities. You only 'love' love when it is easy and simple and uncomplicated. But real adult relationships are work, and long-term love is hard. You have to give it your all. You must really want it. You have to be in it one hundred percent."

She let go of his chin and, not seeing the remorse in his eyes that she was looking for, she crossed her arms and added, "You've never been in a mature relationship before, so believe me when I tell you that this is how it is. Stay in this relationship and you'll learn. You will understand. Don't give up now. Please."

"Really?" Luca said, meeting her eyes. "None of that sounds right to me. I understand that everything good requires effort and commitment, but love, of all things, should *not* be hard. You shouldn't have to force yourself to love someone. Right now, I am not feeling it at all. This relationship feels like a job."

"So, you are going to throw two years away just like that?" Maria asked, taking half a step back. "Walk away when you don't 'feel it' anymore? That's so incredibly immature! It only confirms that you don't know what real love is. It is not the stupid, flowery, over-the-top romantic poems you study in your literature classes. Those are just pipe dreams written by some drunk or drug-addled ancient poet trying to make money. They were all dreamers just trying to use pretty words to wish something into being. Have you ever *really* loved anything in your life? Anything you would give your whole being for and commit your life to?"

He looked at her and quietly replied, "Yes, absolutely. Baseball. I have always loved the game."

Her laugh exploded in his face. "Baseball?" she responded derisively. "You're so shallow. You sound like you're twelve years old. You can't compare a relationship to a *game*!"

"Maybe not," he replied, turning from her to pick up his bat bag, "but that's how I feel. I love the game. I love the idea of it, the feel of it, even the smell of it. I know it's where my future lies and where my dreams will come true. I don't have to struggle with not wanting to play it. The desire is *always* there. Maybe I don't have room in my heart for anything else right now, and maybe someday I will regret it, but right now it is what I want—what I need."

"Then go!" she screamed pushing him away, starting to cry. "Go. Go play your game. Go play your stupid, childish game. And when it breaks your heart, don't come running back to me." She turned to walk away, then suddenly stopped and turned back toward him, looking deflated. "I could compete against another girl, or even a job or career, but I can't compete with an idea, a concept, a set of rules. When all your immature dreams become a nightmare, and you find yourself a lonely old man, remember that you could have had something real, something meaningful, and you threw it away for a stupid game. I can't believe that I thought we could ever have a life together."

Her tears escalating to hysterical sobs, Maria turned and ran back toward her dorm. Luca instinctively took a step to follow her, but something stopped him this time. He couldn't take the next step as he had so many times before. Luca stood there frozen, heart beating wildly, mind racing, unable to tell if what he was feeling was a sudden deep sense of loss or the wild exhilaration of freedom.

As he stood there in the parking lot trying to understand, time seemed to stop. Her words kept running through his mind like an echo of the future. He knew he could fix everything by going to her dorm room now and telling her that he was sorry, that he was wrong, and that he had just lost his mind for a moment and she was right. He could fight through all it would cost him emotionally and make it work for her sake. He could tough it out, but he knew that it would still be a lie. To live out that lie every day would cost him a huge part of himself, forever.

For the first time in his life, Luca decided to go with the truth he knew in his heart and stick with it, despite the fact that someone he cared about would be terribly hurt. It was over, and it needed to stay that way.

He opened the door of his car, threw his bat bag into the back seat, and headed to practice. The season was almost over and, as captain, he didn't want to ruin his perfect on-time record. As he walked into the locker room to change into his practice uniform, his mind shifted into baseball mode and he couldn't help but think, man, I love this game.

CHAPTER TWO

───◇───

"Luca Milano! My office, now!" bellowed the head coach as he stormed through the locker room, not even looking at him.

"What did you do?" asked Tommy Hank, Luca's best friend, co-captain, and roommate. "He sounds pissed off."

"No idea," replied Luca as he pulled on his t-shirt and gathered his books. "I guess I'll find out soon enough." He closed his locker, took a deep breath, and headed to the coach's office.

"Do you want me to wait for you, or should I meet you at home?" asked Tommy. Luca disappeared through the door without answering him.

"Close the door," Coach Shane instructed, leaning back in his chair and putting his feet up on his desk.

"What's up, coach? What's going on?" asked Luca as he nervously seated himself in the chair across from him.

"We have five games left and I need you to commit to keeping your focus," said Coach Shane. "We have a shot at the NCAA playoffs this year, and these last five games could make a huge difference in our seeding. As captain, nothing is more important than you setting the example for the team. I need you to drive them and yourself right through to the end. Understood?"

"Of course, coach," replied Luca, extremely confused. "I'm always focused, and I take my position seriously; you know that. Why are you bringing this up now?"

"Because of this," Coach Shane said, and threw a manila envelope across the desk at Luca.

It looked like one of those envelopes that the dean used to send the team's grades to the coach or that could contain legal documents of some sort. Luca grabbed the envelope and thought, man, I must have really screwed up on that accounting final. Did I pay that last parking ticket I got in Philly?

As he removed the documents that were inside, his mind was racing so fast that he couldn't focus. All he saw was a logo, which did not immediately register with him. "What is this, coach?" he asked, still confused.

"It's an offer letter," the coach replied. "You've been drafted in the fifteenth round by the Braves. If you sign, you report to the Durham Bulls in North Carolina, in the Carolina League, as soon as the NCAA playoffs are done. That's assuming you sign that offer today and don't break any bones between now and then."

Luca was dumbstruck. He knew that he was being considered for the draft after having a great junior year and an even better senior year, but still, he never really let himself believe it would happen.

Hardly anyone from Villanova ever got drafted, since they had such a weather-shortened season every year. They just didn't have the notoriety that was usually necessary for serious consideration.

"How, coach? I mean, why? None of the scouts seemed all that interested in me, and when I spoke with them, they were all so lukewarm. I really thought that I had no shot."

"But you had me," Coach Shane replied. "Look, I know a lot of people in the game, and they trust me. I put my reputation on the line for you. I have watched you grow since you walked onto this team. You impressed me from the first time I saw you. Even without a scholarship, you hustled more than anyone else I have ever had. You waited your turn, never complained about playing time, always hustled, and did anything I asked of you. You were rough when you came here—really raw talent—but you took every bit of advice and used it to get better. Your growth has been exponential, and I am convinced you are not done growing as a ballplayer. As good as you are now, I believe you will be even better. What the Braves are buying is your potential. That is what I sold them on, don't make a liar out of me."

"*You* did this?" asked Luca. "I don't know how to thank you, coach!"

"Just keep your head in the game until we are done and that will be thanks enough," replied Coach Shane as he stood from his chair, hand extended. "And remember to help some other kid someday when you are in the position to do so. Pay it forward. That's what we do in this game."

Luca grabbed his hand and pumped it so hard that Coach Shane had to use his other hand to pull himself free.

"I will, coach, I will, for sure. Thank you, thank you so much!"

When Luca got out into the locker room, it was empty except for Tommy, who had decided to wait for him. "So, how did it go? Are you still captain?"

"Yeah," said Luca, "everything is great, but I have one question for you. Do you know where Durham, North Carolina is?"

CHAPTER THREE

———————◇———————

Summer 1980

"Samantha Jolene Jackson! Come in here right now!" yelled her mama as she stood on the back porch, holding another baseball that had found its way through her kitchen window.

Sammi Jo, hiding behind the shed with her cousin Pat once again, knew that this time might be the final straw. She had just finished paying the price for the window she broke two weeks ago, and she knew her mama was going to be furious.

"You'd better go," said Pat. "She knows that this is where we hide when this happens, and if she has to come and find you, it's going to be worse for you. You'd better give yourself up now. Just don't tell her I was the one pitching!"

"Sure," said Sammi Jo, "I'm sure she is going to believe that I hit the ball that far while pitching to myself. She knows we always play together, and you are just a guilty as I am. Come with me."

"No way!" Pat exclaimed. "I'd rather face her wrath after she's taken most of it out on you. I'm taking the back way home. I might even stop at Granny's house so she can't find me for a while. See ya!"

Sammi Jo frowned as she watched Pat run through the backyard to their grandmother's house, knowing there was no escape. She had to turn herself in once again.

Sammi Jo took a deep breath and yelled, "Coming, Mama!"

Leaving her bat and glove behind the shed, she hustled to the back porch. When she got there, her mother was sitting in a kitchen chair holding the baseball she had hit through the window. It looked like she was praying.

"Sorry, Mama" said Sammi Jo. "I was behind the shed and didn't hear you the first time. Why are you praying? Is something wrong?"

"Yes, something's wrong!" exclaimed her mother. "You're fifteen years old now, and you should be becoming more ladylike. Instead, you're spending your summer playing baseball, fishing, and riding your bike who knows where. When are you going to become more like your sister Savannah? By the time she was your age, she would never have been caught dead playing baseball with the boys or going fishing. And she certainly did not hit baseballs through my kitchen window every other week! Sammi Jo, you really need to put this all behind you and start finding ladylike things to occupy your time. Now, go into the kitchen, clean up all the broken glass, then go to your room until your father comes home. I think he needs to have a serious talk with you. I am going to sit here for a while and pray for you. Maybe you should send up some prayers yourself! Now go."

Sammi Jo cleaned up the glass on the kitchen floor, then went to her room, all the while thinking about what her mother had said.

What did she want her to do? Stop being her? Start being Savannah? She would rather die. She loved being outdoors and doing all sorts of fun things. What did it

9

matter if she played with the boys? She was better than them, and they didn't seem to mind. Besides, when they were playing baseball, things were not weird with boys. It was when things got quiet that the boys got weird. Savannah seemed to like when boys got weird.

Sammi Jo actually couldn't wait until her father got home because she knew that he would understand. He was always on her side and loved that they could go fishing on the weekends, work in the yard together, and even play catch after he came home from work. Some of her best memories were when she and her dad were off somewhere in the woods or out on the lake together.

She laughed to herself as she remembered the night they went frog gigging. It was just the two of them and it was pitch black on the big pond at daddy's family's old homeplace. They were just floating out there, not far from the bank, listening for frogs, and when they heard one near the boat, she would snap on the flashlight and her daddy would gig the frog.

It was great fun, until the snakes showed up. For some reason, the pond was especially infested with them that summer. As they floated on the water, they were surrounded by the biggest water moccasins Sammi Jo had ever seen. They were attracted to the light and were trying to get into the boat. Sammi Jo had never seen her father panic like that before. He grabbed the light from her and turned it on.

When he saw all the snakes trying to get into the boat, he actually suggested they jump into the water to swim to shore. She quickly reminded him that there were more snakes in the water than in the boat and that he would be jumping into their territory. He decided she was right, and they desperately rowed for shore, trying to outrun the snakes.

After pulling the boat onto the bank, they ran to the car and sat there for almost an hour laughing so hard they cried. That was maybe her best memory ever. She would *never* give that up for anything. Especially not to be like Savannah.

Sammi Jo heard her daddy drive up and slam the truck door. She watched through her bedroom window as her mama met him in the driveway and spoke with him. Soon, there was a knock on the door.

"Sammi Jo, are you in there? Can I come in?" her daddy asked.

She ran to the door, flung it open, and before he could say anything, hugged him tight. "Daddy," she started, "I'm so sorry about the window, Pat and I were playing in the backyard and I really tagged one. I never thought it would hit the house, but it did. I will pay for it again. Just don't make me be like Savannah, please. Just let me be me!"

Her father had a smile on his face as he guided her to her bed and sat her down. He pulled the chair from her desk, turned it around to face her, and sat.

"Sweetie, just calm down. Nobody is going to make you be Savannah," he reassured her. "We like you just the way you are."

"Mama doesn't," Sammi Jo insisted. "She hates me. She's embarrassed by me. She says 'why can't you be like Savannah? Why do you dress like a boy? Why don't you put a little makeup on, honey? The boys like that.' She wants to turn me into something I'm not. You like me this way right, Daddy? You love me, don't you?"

"Of course, I do," he responded gently, "and so does Mama. Look, Sammi Jo, you are at an age where most girls *want* to dress up and put on makeup and do girly things. Mama is just trying to offer those things to you, not force them on you. She cares about you and just wants what's best for you, and so do I. But if you are not ready for them, then that's okay, too. We both love you very much and want you to be *you*, not Savannah. But I have to say that there is nothing wrong with Savannah. She just prefers things that you do not. Things you don't yet understand. Soon you will, but that has to come in its own time. There's a lot you can learn from your sister if you just open your heart to her a bit. She's not as shallow as you think she is."

"Really?" replied Sammi Jo. "Have you noticed how much time she takes in the bathroom? Or how prissy she is about her clothes? Did you see her at church last Sunday getting all goofy around Jimmy Simmons? It made me want to puke!"

By this time, her father was laughing so hard that it made Sammi Jo start laughing too. "Can you imagine her on a frog gigging trip?" he asked. "She would have been worse than me! I guarantee she would have turned the boat over and drowned us all trying to get away from those snakes!"

By now they were both laughing so hard they had tears in their eyes. That's when her mother poked her head into the room.

"What in the world is going on in here?" she asked, looking sternly at her husband. "Henry, I sent you in here to talk to her about breaking my windows every other week, and here I find you both laughing it up. Is this discipline? I don't think so! You two are so alike, two peas in a pod. I give up!" She slammed the door and left both of them there, doubled up in laughter, enjoying their time together and becoming even closer.

When the laughing stopped, her father pulled three tickets out of his pocket and said, "Look, Sammi Jo, I have an idea. I have three tickets here for the Durham Bulls game this weekend. I thought that you and I and Mama could go, but now that I don't think Mama is going to be talking to either of us for a while, why don't we take Savannah with us? It would be good for you to be around each other outside of just home and church. You might see a different side of her. What do you think? Do you want to go?"

"Of course, I want to go!" said Sammi Jo, jumping off the bed and hugging her daddy once again. "I *love* the Bulls. Even if Savannah is there, as long as you are, too, I know I'll have fun. Thank you, Daddy. I can't wait!"

CHAPTER FOUR

Sitting there on the long bus ride back to Durham, Luca was rethinking his decision to sign with the Bulls. It was different than the vision he'd had of what professional baseball was going to be like. Of course, he had been to a lot of minor league games growing up, but being in the stands, and seeing the game and all the fun interactive activities at minor league parks, gives you a completely different impression than what it is really like for the ballplayers. The travel was absolutely the worst part.

At Villanova, they'd traveled a bit, but it was only for a couple of days at a time. A few hours to play Navy at Annapolis or Army at West Point. Then a few trips to play St. John's and Seton Hall in New York and New Jersey. Never too long, and back then it always felt like an adventure. Even when they went to Florida for spring training and had to sleep four to a room or on cots at the Detroit Tigers complex in Lakeland, it was still all fun and games.

He never imagined the drudgery and monotony of minor league travel; it seemed endless. On the road for weeks at a time, always trying to sleep or keep your mind occupied while riding the bus. Worst of all, it always seemed to be at night when you couldn't even watch the scenery pass by. A few months into this new career and it was already getting old. He felt like he was always playing tired. His only consolation was that at least he was playing well. That was the easy part.

Coach Shane had been right. These coaches all knew so much more than the college coaches, and he was learning more and more every day and loved it. He could never have imagined how much more he had to learn, and it excited him to think that he still had so much upside. He was determined to maximize his potential and not embarrass Coach Shane. That is, if he could endure the travel part of it all.

That, and the food.

Luca came from a huge Italian family. Food was life to all of them, and they made an art of it. Here in the south, food was just weird. Grits? Collard greens? Pickled pigs' feet? They ate like barbarians, roasting whole pigs and ripping the meat from the steaming animal carcass. "Pig picking", they called it.

It had been ages since he'd had a good bowl of pasta, or even a decent slice of pizza. For Pete's sake, how hard was it to make pizza? He couldn't even get a decent meatball sandwich. *Meatballs!* Meat in the shape of a ball! How much more basic can you get than that? Even that simple culinary delight seemed way beyond the capacity of the genius chefs in the south. He had to settle for meatloaf, which had been his go-to meal for the past month. What scared him was that he was beginning to like it. Things were definitely going downhill.

While his mind tortured him over all these trivial issues there in the dark on the hot and fetid bus, he remembered the letter he got from Tommy Hank last week before they left on the most recent road trip. Tommy had been great at staying in touch since graduation. He wrote almost every week and called at least once a month. He was a really great friend and seemed interested in everything Luca was doing.

Luca pulled the letter out of his bag and began to read.

He laughed as soon as he opened it. *"Batman."* That was Tommy's dual-purpose nickname for him because of his obsession with Batman, the comic book hero, and his skills with a baseball bat.

Hey Batman,

Still killing it there in Durham? Last time we talked, you were leading the team in batting average and RBIs. Just like old times, huh? Loved hearing about the trip to Lynchburg. Seriously, bar fights at your age? Aren't you supposed to be a mature professional now? You can't go getting all crazy just because some hayseed called you "pretty boy". He probably meant it as a compliment! Well, maybe not.

Anyway, just relax and enjoy the ride, you have the whole world in the palm of your hand. Don't go getting yourself busted up in a bar fight when the major leagues are just around the corner. You'll be there in no time.

Just stay healthy, keep learning, and find yourself a nice Southern girl to have some fun with, and time will pass quickly. Seriously, don't screw this up! I am counting on you.

Tommy

P.S. Ray Porecca says hello. Saw him and Coach Fidalgo last week at an alumni event. Ray is getting married next fall and Phil will be his best man. BIG surprise, huh?

Luca put the letter back in the envelope and thought, yeah, the majors are right around the corner. I hope I can endure all of this until then.

CHAPTER FIVE

The Bulls were playing at home against the Lynchburg Mets, and in theory, it should be an easy game. But after a week on the road with hardly any sleep, Luca felt like crap.

He walked into the locker room at El Toro Stadium feeling like he was fifty years old. The fact that the stadium was just about that old itself enhanced the feeling. But he really loved this old stadium. From the first time he walked on the field, he was struck by the palpable sense of history the stadium evoked in him.

It hadn't changed much in the forty years since it was built, with the low, cozy stands, the unique and distinctive conical ticket tower, the garish blue and orange colors, the local tobacco advertisements covering the outfield wall, and the smell of freshly cut grass mixing with decades of old tobacco juice. It all transported him back to the days of Ty Cobb and Honus Wagner, and no matter how bad he felt when he arrived, by the time he suited up, he was ready to play.

The excitement and thrill of lacing up his spikes, grabbing his glove, and hustling onto the always-green field was the same one he had felt since he was seven years old. It never changed. That is what he had tried to make Maria understand the day they stood there in the parking lot at school, breaking up. This, to him, was love. It never changed. It was always exciting and new, never diminishing.

Sure, there were challenges and hard work, bad times and good times, ups and downs, pain and difficulty surrounding it all, but his love of the game never diminished. It was fresh and alive every time he stepped on the field. For him, that defined love. If he was ever going to have another relationship, that was what he wanted—an enduring, passionate, evergreen love.

Luca wrote poetry during the long, dreary bus rides to those small, uninteresting cities. It was something he had developed a passion for over the years, but he had never told anyone about it, mostly because the guys he played with would never understand. He had been introduced to poetry by his father's lifelong love of it. He would sit with Luca, his brother, and sister on cold, snowy winter nights and read classic poems to them by the fireplace in the living room. He read with passion and animation, emphasizing certain passages, and explaining the meaning of the poem when he was done. He connected each poem to real life, making the meaning and focus of the work come alive for them.

From that point on, Luca began to see life differently than his peers. Poetry touched a part of him that was so different from his athletic life. One was so physical, the other so emotional. Over the years, his twin passions became intertwined to a point that he could not separate them now. He saw baseball in terms of poetry and poetry in baseball terms. The beauty of a majestic home run, the poignancy of a disputed play at the plate, the ballet-like movements of turning a double play—he could write poetic verses about all of them.

He wished relationships could be like that. He longed

for a relationship filled with the poetic beauty that he saw in the game and with the passion he felt when he was playing it.

Maybe someday, he thought as he did his stretching exercises, but not today. Today it was all about the game— one hundred percent, no distractions.

He finished stretching and found someone to warm up with as the stands started to fill with early arrivals. Between warm up throws, he scanned the stadium and noted that the local people were so different than those he grew up with in the northeast. These people seemed more relaxed and open. They exuded a friendly and affable sensibility so unlike the agitated animation he had always sensed in the crowds he played in front of in New York.

Even at high school games, there had always seemed to be conflict in the stands and irritation at the umpires, coaches, and players. Very few people seemed to be there just for the enjoyment of seeing a well-played game. Here, everyone seemed content to just drink in the atmosphere and enjoy the experience. The players were usually unknown to them, so they weren't here for them. They were here for themselves and their families. They wanted to relax in the enjoyment of a game that embodied all that was good about the sport and the country.

It has been said that baseball is a metaphor for life, and Luca truly believed that. That made sense to him. Since that was true, maybe local baseball fans were a metaphor for the area in which they lived? Maybe minor league fans were a metaphor for a small hometown life versus the big city metaphor of the major leagues. That also seemed to make sense in the poetic part of Luca's mind. He kind of liked it in this rural town, but it was not for him. He was going to make it to the big time, in life and in love. There would be no living in obscurity for him. That was one thing he was sure of.

As he was returning to the dugout from finishing his sprints in the outfield, he heard his name being called. When he looked to where it was coming from, standing there, leaning out over the railing of the box seats along the first base line, was someone he never thought he would see again—the giant hayseed guy from the bar in Lynchburg.

"Hey, pretty boy!" he taunted. "Yeah, you. New York pretty boy!" Luca stopped and stared at him, completely taken out of his pregame thoughts. "You better know that I'm watching you today, and I'm gonna torture you the whole game. Then when it's done, I'm gonna beat the snot outta you!" the huge man warned.

Luca tipped his hat to him, continued to the dugout, and thought, yep, minor league fans are definitely a metaphor for small town life.

CHAPTER SIX

———◇———

Sammi Jo, Savannah, and their father, Henry, got to the stadium early so Sammi Jo could watch batting practice. Her dad knew that she loved to examine the various batting stances and to analyze the unique swings of all the players. It was one of the things he loved about her.

She was always so full of life and intensely interested in the details of it. She would analyze everything and then incorporate the best parts of what she learned into her own activities. Always searching, always learning, she yearned to improve, to be better at everything. He often wondered if that showed a lack of confidence in herself or dissatisfaction with who she was.

Savannah had no such dissatisfaction. She was supremely comfortable in her own skin, never showing any desire to be anything but herself. It was as if she felt that she had emerged into the world perfectly formed, just waiting for the world to acknowledge her perfection. As she sat there, disinterested and distracted, apparently annoyed at being dragged to a boring baseball game on a beautiful, sunny summer Saturday, Sammi Jo elbowed her. With a mouth full of popcorn, she said "'Vannah, see that guy in the batting cage? I bet he pops up at least three times today. He's dropping his back shoulder every time he swings. Just watch, his back elbow is collapsing."

Savannah rolled her eyes and watched. "I don't see anything," she said fanning herself because of the heat. "He looks like all the others. Frankly, I hope they all strike out every time so we can go home early."

"Well, I hope it goes into extra innings," replied Sammi Jo. "I could stay here all day. Can't you feel the excitement? That's what I love about baseball," she continued, ignoring her sister's obvious disinterest. "You never know what's going to happen. The game could go on forever! There is no clock, no time limit. Sure, every game will eventually end, but nobody knows when ahead of time. That's part of why I love the game so much."

Her father leaned over, grabbed a handful of Sammi Jo's popcorn, and added, "I agree, it's great that baseball has no clock, no time limit or 'sudden death' overtime. You know there is an end to the game, but never exactly when. In baseball, just like in life, we often fight the hardest in the last inning of the game when we are down to our last strike. Nothing is ever final until the last strike. I like that; you can always stay in the game if you just keep swinging and keep your eye on the ball."

Savannah wrinkled up her nose and said to Sammi Jo, not daring to address her father, "When did you become so philosophical? You're just a dumb kid who doesn't even know how to dress her age. Just shut up and let me suffer through this game in silence, please."

"Sammi Jo, come over here and sit by me and leave your sister alone," said Henry, standing to slide over one seat to separate the girls. "Let her enjoy the game in her own way."

Sammi Jo gathered up her popcorn, glove, and program, and as she moved to take her seat on the opposite side of her dad, the national anthem started.

She stood still where she was, shoved everything under her left arm and put her right hand over her heart. She faced the flag in centerfield and watched as all the players removed their caps and did the same. As the anthem was playing, her eyes fell on the shortstop.

He was new this year, and she had read that he was having a great year. It said in the program that he was from New York. She liked the way he moved during infield practice, gliding around and fielding ground balls effortlessly. He was smooth and graceful and had a great arm, but he was the one dropping his shoulder in batting practice. Another "great field, no hit" shortstop, she thought, just like all the others before him. The anthem ended, and she took her seat next to her dad.

As she was arranging her belongings, a guy in front of them started yelling at the shortstop. "Hey *Looooka*, what kinda name is that? Go back to New York where all them other pretty boys are. You stink! You're gonna get your Yankee butt kicked today, and I'm gonna love it."

Henry leaned forward and spoke softly in the man's ear. "Excuse me, but I have my two young daughters with me today, and I would appreciate it if they didn't have to listen to you shooting your mouth off all game long. So please, watch your language and keep it down."

The huge man, irritated by the request, replied, "Then don't none of y'all listen. I'm gonna ride that Yankee all nine innings. If y'all don't like it, then find another seat."

Sammi Jo leaned closer to her dad and said, "Don't worry about it, Daddy, it's all part of the game. I don't care about it. Let's just enjoy the game. I love these seats, and I don't want to move. We've never had seats so close to the field before, and we're just behind first base, we can see all the action!"

Luca could hear the hayseed riding him as he fielded the warmup ground balls from the first baseman. Worst of all, he could see his enormous red face right over the first baseman's shoulder every time he threw to him. That was going to be a distraction that he was going to have to deal with the whole game.

"Play ball!" said the umpire, and the leadoff batter stepped into the batter's box.

Instantly, all thoughts about his country boy nemesis evaporated. That's the way it had always been. As soon as he heard that first pitch pop the catcher's glove, he was in the zone. Nothing had ever been able to break through his focus before when he was on the field.

The inning went quickly, with two strikeouts and an infield ground ball to second base. He hustled off the field and grabbed his bat and helmet, since he was in the number two hole today. As he stepped into the on-deck circle, he heard the hayseed from Lynchburg taunting him. "*Looooka*! Hey, stupid *Loooka*! You're gonna strike out because you swing like a girl!"

Luca ignored him and took his practice swings, adding a little pine tar to his bat and studying the pitcher, determined that nothing was going to break his concentration. He was having a great year, and he wasn't going to let some crazy fan rattle him.

The leadoff batter singled to left on the second pitch, and Luca knocked the dirt from his spikes before advancing into the batter's box. He dug in and waited for the first pitch. He loved jumping on the first pitch in his first at bat of a game. Most pitchers assumed that early in the game, batters would want to see as many pitches as possible to get used to the pitcher's rhythm. Not Luca. He believed that early in the game, pitchers would be trying to get a feel for the mound and would be throwing mostly fastballs. This guy had only thrown two pitches so far and seemed to be struggling getting used to the mound. Luca focused on the spot the ball would be coming from just above the pitcher's right shoulder and waited. As soon as the ball was released, he knew it was a juicy fastball, right down the middle. He swung viciously and popped it up. Disgusted with the result, he slammed the bat down and hustled to first base.

As he turned to head back to the dugout after the play was made, he heard the hayseed laughing, "See, I told ya. You stink, *Loooka*. You swing like a girl. My sister can hit better than you!" He shot the guy a glance and kept moving.

The game progressed, and so did the taunting. The Bulls were ahead three to two late in the top of the ninth inning, but Luca was zero for three with three popups and was not a happy camper. He could feel himself getting more frustrated as the game wore on. He was actually beginning to believe what the Lynchburg hayseed was saying; he *did* stink, at least today anyway. One more out, and this nightmare would be over. From his position at shortstop, he focused on home plate as the pitcher began his wind up.

The batter hit a screaming one hop grounder to the hole between shortstop and third base. Taking one quick crossover step and diving to his right, he speared the grounder backhanded, got up in one smooth motion and drew back to make the throw to first base. The first thing he saw was the huge, ugly red face of the hayseed right over the right shoulder of the first baseman. He gritted his teeth and rifled the ball.

It sailed on him.

The first baseman leaped to make the play, but the ball tipped off the top of his glove. He watched in horror as the ball rocketed into the stands and smashed the hayseed right in the face. The ball deflected off the hayseed's cheekbone and hit the girl sitting behind him to his right, bouncing off her forehead. What a mess! After the runner arrived at second base because of the overthrow, Luca stood there with him, looking into the stands, assessing the damage.

"Nice throw," the runner said. "I'm glad you finally shut that guy up. He was really getting on my nerves."

"I just wish I had actually meant it," Luca replied. "At least I would have gotten some satisfaction from it."

Some of the medical personnel were escorting the hayseed to the medical tent while others were attending to the girl, who appeared to be semi-conscious. Play resumed, and the next batter flew out to center, ending the game. Luca couldn't remember the last time he was so happy to be done with a game. Oh for three, three popups, and a wild throwing error. He definitely needed some sleep and maybe some extra batting practice tomorrow.

CHAPTER SEVEN

———◇———

"Daddy, is Savannah going to be all right?" asked Sammi Jo as the attendants held ice packs on her sister's head.

"Yes, she'll be fine. She'll have that huge bump on her forehead for a while, but there's no permanent damage," her father replied. "Let's just sit here while the crowd leaves so we don't have to drag her through everyone."

As they sat there ministering to Savannah, Luca came over to where they were sitting. "Look, Daddy," Sammi Jo said, "it's the shortstop who threw the ball."

Henry leaned toward Luca. "Nice throw, son," he remarked sardonically.

Luca looked sheepishly at him. "I'm really sorry about that. I don't normally have throwing errors. I guess I got distracted by that guy in front of you. He was riding me all game."

"I'm glad he got his comeuppance," said Henry. "If you didn't bust his nose, I was about to. So, you saved me some aggravation."

"Is that your daughter? Will she be all right?" asked Luca as Savannah perked up a bit.

"Outside of that huge bump on her forehead, she'll be fine," Henry replied. "Thanks for checking on her, son, it shows real class."

"Could you sign my baseball?" interrupted Sammi Jo, holding the blood-stained baseball out for Luca to see. "It's the first baseball I have ever caught at a game and I want to remember this day forever!"

"Sure," Luca said with a laugh. "But wouldn't you rather have a new one? I can go get one of the other game balls for you. You don't have to keep that one all covered in blood."

"Are you kidding? This one is great!" exclaimed Sammi Jo. "No one else will ever have one like it. Just sign it, okay?"

As Sammi Jo handed him the baseball and the pen she was using to keep score, Luca asked, "What do you want it to say?"

"Just say 'To Sammi Jo, Love, Luca. Keep swinging for the fences.'"

"Okay," Luca replied, smiling, "anything else?" he asked as he signed the ball.

"Yeah," said Sammi Jo, "and put the date on it."

As Luca signed the ball for Sammi Jo, Savannah shooed away the attendants who were holding ice to her head. She sat forward and extended her hand, "Hi, I'm Savannah. You know, the one you beaned? It's a pleasure to make your acquaintance."

Luca finished signing the baseball, handed it back to Sammi Jo, and took Savannah's hand. This was the first time he had gotten a really good look at her, since previously her face had been covered with ice packs. He seemed enthralled.

"Very pleased to meet you, Savannah. I'm Luca Milano. Sorry about the throw. Are you okay?"

"I am," Savannah replied, looking dreamily into his eyes, "and getting better by the minute."

Luca looked entranced as he stared into her blue eyes. "I would like to invite you all back for tomorrow's doubleheader to make up for all of this," he said. "That way, you can really enjoy a game without having some knucklehead in front of you ruining it for you. If you get here early enough, you can come down onto the field during batting practice and meet some of the players. There'll be tickets waiting for you at the ticket booth under my name. Would you like that?"

Sammi Jo exclaimed, "Yes! Daddy can we come, please?"

"I don't know, Sammi Jo," her father replied. "After all, tomorrow is Sunday, and we have church." Then he turned to Luca. "What time does the first game start?"

"Not until two p.m.," Luca replied. "If you can get here around one, I can show you around."

"Well, I think we can make that work," said Henry, then he smiled. "That is, if the pastor keeps it short tomorrow." He looked at Savannah, who was still holding Luca's outstretched hand, and asked, "Savannah, would you be okay with that?"

Savannah, still looking dreamily at Luca, replied, "Absolutely, Daddy, you know how much I *love* baseball!" Sammi Jo rolled her eyes and stuck her finger down her throat, pretending to gag.

Her dad said to Luca, "You have a deal, son. We'll see you tomorrow at one."

"Great!" said Luca struggling to extricate his hand from Savannah's grip, "One it is, Mr…"

"Jackson." Henry finished, holding out his hand for a shake. "Henry Jackson."

"Mr. Jackson," Luca repeated, accepting the proffered hand, "and you already know my name. I'll see you all tomorrow!" He headed back to the locker room.

As they watched him run across the field, Savannah sighed. "Isn't he *cute*?"

Sammi Jo replied, "He would be a lot cuter if he would stop dropping his back shoulder and get some hits once in a while." That made Henry laugh.

"Well," he said to Savannah, "it looks like you have made a miraculous recovery. I guess baseball must agree with you."

"Not baseball, Daddy," replied Savannah. "Baseball players."

Sammi Jo was horrified. "See Daddy, didn't I tell you? She gets *weird* around boys."

"You will, too, Sammi Jo," observed her dad. "Just not today. Let's get our stuff and head back to the truck. Mama will probably be wondering if we're ever coming home."

When they arrived home, Sammi Jo gushed about everything that happened at the game. When she showed her mama the signed ball, her mother replied, "Well I *certainly* hope that bloody baseball does not end up in my kitchen!"

Sammi Jo, horrified, replied, "Mama, I would never play with this ball. I am going to keep it forever! And I don't want anyone else touching it."

"I don't think that's something you need to worry about," her dad responded. "You can have it all to yourself, blood, dirt, and all."

As Sammi Jo left the room to place her prize in a very prominent position in her room, her mama turned to Henry and said, "Henry, that girl really needs to grow up. Stop encouraging such childish behavior. She's fifteen, only five years younger than Savannah, but you would never know it. You are not doing her any favors by encouraging her to behave this way."

"Relax, Violet," Henry soothed as he hugged her

tightly. "Always remember what a gift she is to this family. Remember how we thought we could never have another child after you lost our boy? That pregnancy was so hard on you, and to have lost him at birth was devastating for both of us. That boy had a lot of our hopes and dreams wrapped up in his tiny, premature body. Even the doctors told us that it wasn't possible for you to get pregnant again. Then along came Sammi Jo out of the blue. Remember what a blessing we felt she was? She's still a blessing. She makes me laugh every day. She makes both of us laugh every day; come on, Violet, admit it! I don't want to ruin what we have or force her to grow up before she's ready. Let her be who she is. She has her own reasons for how she is, and she'll be grown and gone before you know it. Enjoy this time with her, because once it's gone, you are going to miss it. Trust me."

He kissed Violet on the cheek and changed the subject. "Now, how about some of that millionaire pie you have in the fridge? That would taste pretty good about now."

"Okay," Violet sighed. "Call the girls; they love it, too."

CHAPTER EIGHT

The next day, Sammi Jo was up and dressed thirty minutes earlier than on any other Sunday. As she waited at the kitchen table, her dad walked in to get some coffee.

"You're up and dressed unusually early, Sammi Jo," he remarked.

"Yes, Daddy," Sammi Jo replied. "And what is taking everyone else so long? We have to get to church, and I don't want to be late."

"We won't be late," responded Henry. "We will be right on time, as usual. Are you worried that if we're late, it will make the pastor start the services later? When has that ever happened?"

"You never know," said Sammi Jo. "There's a first time for everything, and I don't want it to be today."

Henry chuckled. "Don't worry, Sammi Jo, we will be on time, the pastor will begin on time, and we'll make it to the field by one o'clock, I promise. Just sit there and read your Bible, and the rest of us will be ready in a few minutes."

Sammi Jo randomly opened her Bible and began reading at 1 Corinthians 13:11.

When I was a child, I spoke and thought and reasoned as a child. But when I grew up, I put away childish things.

She closed the Bible and looked up to heaven and prayed. "Even you, God? Has Mama been talking with you about me again? I get it, I know I have to grow up, but does it have to be today? Can you give me a week or so? Or maybe until the end of baseball season? Then I promise I will try. Do we have a deal?"

"Who are you talking to?" asked Savannah as she swept into the kitchen in her special Sunday sundress.

"Just praying," said Sammi Jo. "By the way, I can still see that bump on your head. No amount of makeup is going to cover that!"

"Just be quiet, you little brat," Savannah hissed, "and don't talk about it at church. Just keep your mouth shut. I don't need you pointing it out in front of Jimmy Simmons."

"You still like Jimmy Simmons?" asked Sammi Jo, "The way you got all dreamy-eyed around that Luca guy yesterday, I thought he was your new crush."

"We'll see," said Savannah. "I just like to keep my options open, and I don't need my little sister closing any doors for me. So behave today. Got it?"

"Yeah, yeah, yeah," Sammi Jo replied, rolling her eyes. "I got it."

At church, the services seemed to drag on forever to Sammi Jo. "Stop fidgeting," her mother instructed as she put her hand on Sammi Jo's knee.

"I can't, Mama, the pastor is going to make us late for the game."

"There are more important things than baseball games, Samantha," replied Violet sternly. "Just be patient. You won't be late, I promise."

Sammi Jo, still fidgeting and distracted, looked around the church. She found where her sister was sitting with Jimmy Simmons and his family, and it made her mad. You didn't sit with someone's family at church unless you *really* liked them. And you certainly did not sit with them at church the day after you were making eyes at some ballplayer. That has to be some sort of sin, she thought.

She focused back on the pastor and remembered the verse from 1 Corinthians she had read earlier and thought, when I do decide to put childish things aside, I am never going to be like Savannah. There has to be a way to grow up and still be who I am. If I have to behave like Savannah, I'd rather die! It is so embarrassing.

After what seemed like hours, the pastor finished his sermon, wrapped up the service, and everyone headed for the parking lot.

"Come on, Daddy," urged Sammi Jo, pulling on his arm. "We have to get home and change clothes so we can get to the ballpark."

"Just a minute," replied Henry. "We have to wait for Savannah."

Sammi Jo searched the crowd and spotted Savannah talking with Jimmy Simmons next to his family's truck.

"I'll get her," said Sammi Jo as she ran to where they were.

"Hey, Jimmy," said Sammi Jo as she approached the couple. "Savannah, we have to go. Daddy says to come now."

Savannah shot her a withering look and said, "I'll be there in a minute. Just leave us alone."

That made Sammi Jo mad, so she decided to get even.

"Hey Jimmy, did you notice the huge knot on Savannah's forehead? Pretty gruesome, isn't it? Pretty hard to look at, wouldn't you say?"

As Savannah turned bright red and glared at her younger sister, Jimmy replied, "I hadn't noticed. But now that you mention it, yeah, I do. Savannah, how did you get that?"

Savannah replied, "At some dumb baseball game yesterday that my daddy dragged us to. I got hit with a bad throw that one of those dopey ballplayers made. I'll be fine."

As Jimmy leaned in to examine the injury more closely, Savannah pulled back and said quickly, "Well, I guess I have to go. See you next week, Jimmy."

As she and Sammi Jo walked back to their parents, Savannah said, "That was cruel. Remember, I never forget. Someday, Sammi Jo, I will return the favor."

Sammi Jo just smiled and took off running. "Shotgun!" she shouted, jumping into the front passenger seat of her daddy's truck.

When they arrived at El Toro Park, they got their tickets at the will-call window of the ticket booth. Three tickets were waiting for them, just as Luca had promised, along with a note.

Mr. Jackson, bring the girls to the gate near the dugout on the first base line. I will meet you there. Luca.

"Let's go, girls," said Henry. "Luca will meet us by the dugout. Let's not keep him waiting, or he might miss his turn for batting practice."

"And he sure needs a lot of it," added Sammi Jo.

"What would you know about it?" sneered Savannah, still angry about her sister's stunt at church.

"More than you," was Sammi Jo's reply. "I'm a really good hitter, and I pay attention to what other players do. What Luca is doing is obvious to me. Maybe I will give him a few tips!"

"Don't you dare!" exclaimed Savannah. "You may have already messed up one promising situation today, I don't want you messing up another. Just stay quiet and appreciate the experience."

Sammi Jo responded, "We'll see."

"Daddy, tell her not to say anything to Luca about his swing," pleaded Savannah. "That would be rude and embarrassing."

"Sammi Jo, don't say anything to Luca about his swing," instructed Henry. "Unless, of course, you are asked. Then say anything you want. Understood?"

"Yes, Daddy," said Sammi Jo. "Can I ask him any questions? I am sure there's a lot he can teach me about the game."

"Sure, ask anything you want. Just be respectful. After all, according to the program, he is seven years older than you."

"Any question I want?" asked Sammi Jo.

"Yes," replied Henry as they arrived at the dugout gate. "As long as it's respectful."

"Got it," replied Sammi Jo with a huge smile on her face.

Luca saw them and hustled over from where he was standing at the batting cage. "Glad you could make it," he said to Henry as the two men shook hands. Luca opened the gate and invited them down onto the field. He then stepped into the dugout and returned with three batting helmets.

"Rules say that all visitors on the field during batting practice have to wear these. They might be a little big, but you have to wear them anyway."

Sammi Jo grabbed one immediately and put it on over the Durham Bulls baseball cap she was wearing. "Fits great," she said.

Savannah was holding the helmet that Luca had given her at arm's length with a disgusted look on her face.

"You want me to wear this dirty, used helmet?" she asked.

"That's the deal, Savannah, if you want to be on the field near us," stated Luca.

"Savannah, just put it on so we can go," said her dad. "We're making Luca late for batting practice."

Looking horrified as she did it, Savannah put the oversized helmet on her head, covering her carefully coiffed blonde hair. It also covered her ears, hiding the new hoop earrings she had put on especially for today.

"How is this helpful at all?" she asked Luca as she struggled to position the helmet so that she could see.

"Even though it's a little big, it'll protect you from any foul balls or bad throws," he said with a wink, "and we know what a magnet you are for those!"

Luca led them to the area behind the batting cage. "I'm next," he said, "so excuse me for a few minutes." He returned to the dugout to get his bat and then stepped into the cage and began his swings. He popped up the first two pitches.

"He has a great stance," observed Henry. "Well-balanced and slightly open to allow him to turn on the inside pitches."

"Yeah," said Sammi Jo, "his stance isn't the issue, it's his back shoulder. His whole right side collapses every time he swings."

Luca finished the first ten swings of what he considered an unsatisfactory round of batting practice. He came around the cage and stood with Henry and the girls and watched the next batter.

"Well, that was disappointing," Luca remarked to no one in particular.

"Why do you say that?" asked Sammi Jo.

"Because," said Luca, "I popped up half of them. It

started yesterday and seems to be happening again today. Excuse me for a moment, I need to talk with the batting coach."

"Before you go, can I ask you a question?" asked Sammi Joe as her father and sister held their breath.

"Sure," said Luca, "anything."

"Anything?" Sammi Jo repeated.

"Sure," said Luca, looking puzzled.

Sammi Jo smiled, looked at Savannah and then back to Luca and asked, "Why are you dropping your back shoulder when you swing?"

Savannah's jaw dropped, and Henry put his hand over his face.

"What do you mean, Sammi Jo?" asked Luca.

"I mean your whole right side is collapsing when you stride. Your bat head is dipping, and you are hitting the bottom of the ball every time. Fix that and no more popups!" she said with a smile.

Luca just looked at her for a few seconds without saying anything. His eyes were blinking as he visualized his last round of batting practice. Then his eyes grew wide. "You know what, Sammi Jo, you could be right! Watch me during the next round of BP, and tell me if you are seeing the same thing."

He turned to Henry. "Quite a little batting coach you have here. Did you teach her about the game?"

"A little," replied Henry, "but most of it she picked up on her own. She loves it and reads everything she can about it. She is a real student of the game."

Luca smiled and turned to Sammi Jo. "That's great; I love this game, too. We should stay in touch so I can ask your advice when I get into a slump. That is, if your advice works this time. Let's test it out, it's my turn again."

He stepped into the batting cage, dug in, and wiggled

around a bit, making sure his back shoulder was level with his front shoulder. He popped the first pitch up.

Stepping out of the batter's box, he said to Sammi Jo, "I think I got it. You were right, watch this." He stepped back in, set himself and hit the next pitch to left center field. He turned and winked at Sammi Jo, then proceeded to hit eight more line drives to center.

Sammi Jo was beaming when he finished his turn. "Henry, can I give Sammi Jo a hug? I think she just solved my popup problem!"

"Sure," replied Henry. "I may hug her myself, that was amazing!"

Luca hugged Sammi Jo. "Thanks for the tip," he said. "It was just what I needed to get back on track."

"No problem," Sammi Jo replied. "That's what I do, get things back on track."

"Well, I have to get ready for the game," said Luca. "Your seats are right behind the dugout. Henry, the refreshments are on me today in appreciation for Sammi Jo's advice. I'll tell the kid at the concession stand to see me after the game. Enjoy the game, and I will see you when we're done. I have to get your phone number so I can call my batting coach when I get into trouble." He escorted them to the stands and then said to Savannah, "It was good seeing you again, too, Savannah. Will you be staying until after the games?"

"You can count on it," replied Savannah, smiling for the first time since they'd arrived.

CHAPTER NINE

Luca had a great double header. Three for four in the first game and four for four in the second, with four RBI's and two stolen bases for the day.

Not bad, Luca thought as he got dressed. The kid really knows her stuff. That whole back shoulder thing was right on target. He shook his head and thought, I guess good advice can come from anywhere; sometimes from places you least expect it. We just get off track and are too close to the situation to see what is obvious to others. I hope I am always open to good advice.

He grabbed his things and headed back onto the field to say goodbye to his guests. Seeing them waiting in their seats for him, he picked up his pace.

"Hey Luca, great game," said Henry. "You really tore up the Lynchburg pitching today."

"Yeah, thanks to Sammi Jo's advice," Luca responded. "It was just what I needed to get back on track." He took the program from Sammi Jo and wrote the phone number of the apartment he was renting. He handed it to Henry and said, "Call me anytime you want to come to a game. I get a few free tickets to every home game, and I don't know anyone else here. You'll be my permanent guests, since I think one of you may be my lucky charm!"

"That's great, Luca," replied Henry. "I guess you'll be seeing a lot of us this summer." Then he tore a page from the program and wrote down their phone number, handing it to Luca. "Call us anytime you are in town, I know my wife would love to have you over for dinner sometime, and of course, you may need to consult with your new batting coach," he said, looking at Sammi Jo.

Sammi Jo had a huge smile on her face. Savannah was quiet.

"I will," Luca promised. "Like I said, I don't know anyone here, and I am a long way from home. Some home cooking would be great."

"Wonderful, then I expect to hear from you soon. We will be following your progress in the papers," Henry said as he shook Luca's hand.

"Thank you, Sammi Jo," said Luca, "you really helped me today, and I appreciate it."

"It was easy," replied Sammi Jo. "Really obvious stuff."

Then Luca addressed Savannah, "Did you enjoy the games today?"

Savannah perked up. "Very much so," she replied. "You are a wonderful ballplayer. I can't wait to see you play again."

Luca smiled. "Thanks, that's great to hear. We're heading to Winston-Salem for a few days, but we'll be back playing here next weekend. We have Friday night off. May I call you when I get back? Maybe you can show me a decent restaurant around here."

Savannah just about leaped out of her seat. She looked at her dad and said, "Would that be all right, Daddy?"

Henry smiled. "Sure, sweetie. Luca seems like a very nice boy. I am sure you two will have fun together. I'll vouch for him to your mama, and I'm sure she will be okay with it, too."

Savannah talked all the way home. She chatted with her dad about which restaurants were the best in the Durham area, what would be a good time for him to pick her up, and what she should wear for a dinner with a ballplayer. Sammi Jo just sulked in the back seat.

Henry caught a glimpse of her in the rearview mirror and, noticing her sullen expression, asked, "Sammi Jo, are you feeling all right? I would think you would be happy that your advice was so well received and successful. You may have a future ahead of you as a batting coach!"

"I'm fine," replied Sammi Jo. "I guess I just ate too much free popcorn."

Henry didn't buy it but didn't press the issue.

Luca was happy to be back in his apartment. He had begged off when some of the other players suggested they hit the nightspots in Durham, since he was really worn out and needed some sleep in a real bed. Before he hit the sack, he took out a notebook and started to write.

Since he had joined the Bulls, he had begun recording some bits and pieces from each day, and then when he was on the bus, he would try to craft a poem about some of the experiences. Some were funny, some were melancholy, and some were just about his dreams for the future.

Most people didn't recognize the poetry in everyday life. They just experienced it then let it slip away. One of the things his dad had taught him was that every day, every moment, was a work of art, and every second had beauty. You just had to pay attention and remember. Writing it all down was how Luca remembered. As he scribbled his notes, he wrote about the game, he wrote about Savannah, and he wrote about Sammi Jo.

When he was finished, he turned back to yesterday's page and reviewed his notes about the game and the giant hayseed from Lynchburg and laughed. That was going to be one funny poem when he got a chance to write it. He also thought to himself that it was amazing how life could change in one day. Yesterday, his swing was a mess, he knew no one in town, and was being stalked by a huge country boy. Today, he had made three new friends, had fixed his swing, and found a cute southern girl to hang out with. Things were definitely looking up.

He put down the notebook, got some stationary from the desk, and began to write.

Tommy,
You are not going to believe what happened this weekend...

CHAPTER TEN

Henry got up from his recliner in the living room to answer the phone. "Hello, this is Henry Jackson," he said.

"Hi Mr. Jackson, this is Luca Milano, from the Durham Bulls. I hope it's ok to call this late, but I just got back from Winston-Salem, and I wanted to follow up with Savannah regarding dinner tomorrow night."

"Certainly, Luca," Henry replied. "The girls aren't home yet. Their mama took them shopping, but I expect them home any minute. Can I give Savannah a message?"

"Sure," said Luca. "As long as you and your wife are still okay with it, I would like to pick Savannah up around seven tomorrow night for dinner. I've gotten good recommendations for some places that I think she might enjoy."

"I'm okay with that," Henry said, then chuckled. "You should be aware that it took a little convincing, and I think you may still have some work to do with Violet when you arrive. I'll tell Savannah you called and to be ready around seven." Then he gave Luca the address and directions from Durham and hung up.

As he was returning to his recliner, the door opened and Sammi Jo burst into the house. "Daddy, we had so much fun! Each of us got some new clothes, even Mama!"

Violet followed Sammi Jo into the kitchen, struggling with the bags, and Savannah followed her carrying a few shoe boxes.

"Looks like you guys bought the whole store," Henry said. "I guess you had some success."

"We're not keeping everything," replied Violet. "The girls just could not make up their minds at the store and it was getting late. They're going to take a day or so to decide what to keep, and then I will bring the rest back to Belk's."

"Well, I guess it's good timing," said Henry. "I just got a call from Luca Milano. He left a message that he'll be here tomorrow night around seven to pick up Savannah for dinner. He seems pretty excited."

Savannah dropped the shoe boxes she was carrying. "Really, Daddy? He called here? When?"

"About five minutes ago," replied her dad. "You just missed him. The team just got back from Winston-Salem, and he wanted to make sure we were still okay with it. I told him it was fine."

Violet said, "I am not completely fine with it, Henry. That boy is two years older than Savannah, and I am not sending my girl off on a date with a boy I have never met. I know you said he was nice and respectful, but I have to see it with my own eyes. After all, he is from the North."

"Mama!" exclaimed Savannah, horrified. "Please don't say that when he is here! It could ruin everything."

"I won't say that to him, honey," replied her mama. "I will just assess him in my own way. He'll never know he is being evaluated."

"Daddy, please talk to her and make her be nice to him!" Savannah begged. "You met him; won't Mama take your word for it?"

"Your mama knows how to do this, Savannah, and I'm sure she won't do anything to embarrass you. Why are you getting so upset? Are you even sure *you* like him yet?"

"That's not the point," said Savannah. "Last Sunday, Sammi Jo embarrassed me in front of Jimmy Simmons by pointing out the bump on my forehead. If Mama embarrasses me too, then I may be out of options for the summer. I would like the chance to decide for myself instead of everyone else making the decisions for me."

"You can make your own decisions, and no one is trying to embarrass you," Henry responded, looking pointedly at Sammi Jo. "We just want to make sure he is as nice as he seemed at the ballpark. People behave differently in different situations, and this will be a good test. So just calm down and show me what you bought."

After retreating to their bedrooms to change, the fashion show began. Savannah came out first with a very sweet, buttercup-yellow sundress and some new kitten-heeled, white patent leather summer shoes. She twirled around so her dad could get the full effect.

"This one is my favorite," she said. "Can I keep it Daddy?"

"Sure, sweetie," he replied. "It is very sweet, and I think it is very pretty on you, but I think you need to wear a sweater with it tomorrow in case the restaurant is cold."

"I have one that will go perfectly with this dress," she said, then hugged her dad. "Thank you, Daddy!" she called over her shoulder as she flitted back to her room.

Next, Violet came out with a simple floral shift. Around the waist was a fashionable wide belt, which had a very nice slimming effect, and new low pumps. She also twirled around for effect.

"Wow," said Henry. "You look great, honey! I like that new style! Come over here and give me a hug."

"Henry!" Violet laughed. "Behave! Sometimes you act like a teenage boy." He got up from the recliner and chased her into the kitchen. They were laughing and kidding with each other when Sammi Jo walked into the living room.

"Henry," whispered Violet, pushing him away, "look at Sammi Jo."

Henry turned around and saw Sammi Jo standing there, not moving. She was wearing a light blue pullover-style dress with short sleeves and three buttons at the collar. She had a shiny slim belt around the waist and was barefoot. She started to cry when she saw her dad looking at her.

"What's the matter, sweetie?" her dad asked. "You look wonderful!"

"It's just that it doesn't look the same as it did in the store," Sammi Jo sobbed. "Mama and Savannah got me so excited about buying it, and now I just feel silly, and I can't wear the shoes without tripping!" Then, she ran back into her room and slammed the door.

"Henry, I'll talk with her," said Violet. "This is really the first dress she's had on for something other than church since she was five years old. I really thought she was ready, she seemed so interested in the store. Maybe it's just not time yet."

"But she looked so... pretty!" said Henry. "I was shocked to see her in it, and she looked so much older. Almost like a different girl. Tell her I really like it and give her some confidence. Maybe she'll keep it."

Violet went to Sammi Jo's room and found her sobbing face down on the bed. "Sammi Jo, can we talk?" she asked.

"Mama, what's wrong with me?" said Sammi Jo. "Why can't I feel comfortable wearing these kinds of clothes? All the girls in my school wear stuff like this every day, but I feel so silly dressed this way. I feel like I'm on display or something, or that I'm trying to be someone else. It was fine when it was just you and me and Savannah, but when Daddy looked at me, I just got embarrassed. Why is that?"

Violet went to her and hugged her close. "It's because you love Daddy so much, and you really care about what he thinks of you. You don't want to do anything that will change his opinion of you or change the relationship you have with him. I think you're afraid that if you grow up, he won't treat you the same or do the things with you that you love to share with him. Sammi Jo, look at me."

She took her daughter's tear-stained face in her hands. "Nothing you wear, or anything you do, will change the way he feels about you. He loves you and always will. He doesn't love you just because you play baseball or go fishing or frog gigging together. He loves you for you, and as the years go by, he will love the woman that you are becoming. You have to know that and believe it."

"Are you sure, Mama?" asked Sammi Jo. "Really sure?"

"Absolutely," Violet replied. "In fact, he told me to tell you how pretty you looked in that dress, and that you looked so much older, more mature. Did you see the smile on his face when he saw you? Isn't that what you are always trying to do, put a smile on his face? Your daddy doesn't lie; if he says something, he means it, and so do I. Now, go out there and thank him for the new clothes."

"Okay, Mama," said Sammi Jo as she stood from the bed. "Should I give the new shoes another try?"

"Certainly," her mama responded with a chuckle. "Here, let me help you."

The fashion show continued for the rest of the evening as Henry sat there, obviously enjoying the fun. He looked as though he felt he was the luckiest man on the face of the earth.

CHAPTER ELEVEN

Luca pulled into the gravel driveway of the modest Wake Forest home. The first thing he noticed was how neat and tidy the yard was and how, even though the home was small and simple, it was obviously cared for with love. He also admired the ancient oak trees that lined the driveway. As soon as he had gotten into town, he was struck by the sense of history it evoked in him. He thought about the tract home neighborhood he had grown up in on Long Island. Those homes went back to World War II, but these homes, and much of the town, predated the Civil War. He realized he was really in a different world.

That feeling had been somewhat muted since he had arrived in North Carolina by the other players on the Bulls. Everyone was from somewhere else, and he had felt no real difference from when he played in college and various summer leagues. It was kind of the same thing—everyone was from other states, so they all felt out of place to some degree.

Now, for the first time, he was going to be fully encountering the culture of the south. Meeting people in their own homes was completely different than interacting with them on the neutral turf of the baseball field. He took a deep breath and followed the winding walk to the front door.

Before he could knock, Henry opened the door. "Welcome, Luca, come on in. Would you like some sweet tea? Violet has a magic touch with the stuff. Best in the whole county."

"Sure," said Luca. "I've acquired a taste for sweet tea since I've been here. Thank you."

"Wonderful," replied Henry. "Just sit yourself over there in my chair and Violet will have it for you in a minute." Henry sat on the couch and said, "Savannah is getting ready, so we have a few minutes to catch up. First of all, were the directions okay for you?"

"Yes, sir," said Luca. "No problem. You certainly have a beautiful town. So picturesque and historic. Have you lived here all your life?"

"I have," Henry replied, "except for when I was stationed in Korea in the fifties. Other than that, this has been my family's home for almost one hundred and fifty years."

"Wow," responded Luca, "that is amazing. Those kinds of roots must be a treasure. Have you ever thought of living somewhere else?"

Before Henry could answer, Violet entered the living room from the kitchen carrying a tray with a pitcher and three glasses. She put it on the coffee table and Luca stood.

"So pleased to meet you, Luca; I'm Violet. I have heard so much about you from Henry and the girls. They certainly appreciated your generosity and hospitality at the ballpark."

"It was my pleasure, Mrs. Jackson," replied Luca. "It's so great to know a nice family here, being that I'm so far from home."

Violet poured some sweet tea for all of them and joined Henry on the couch.

Henry continued, "How was the series in Winston-Salem? I read in the papers that you split."

"Yes, sir," replied Luca. "We should have won three of those games, but our bullpen was worn out and let in some late runs in the fourth game."

"And how about your hitting? Still ripping those line drives to center?" asked Henry.

"Yes, sir, still on track," replied Luca as he took a sip of Violet's sweet tea. "Wow," he commented, "this is the best I have ever had! Thanks, Mrs. Jackson, this is a real treat." He took another sip and continued. "Sammi Jo sure set me straight. I am so thankful she spotted the issue with my back shoulder. I could have been in a slump for weeks. Is she around? I would love to thank her again."

"She'll be here soon," Violet answered. "She was over at her cousin Pat's house, but I am sure she wouldn't want to miss seeing you. Savannah will be ready in a few minutes. Since we have some time, tell us about yourself."

"Not much to tell," said Luca. "I'm from New York—Long Island, really. I went to Catholic grammar school, Catholic high school, and then Villanova University. I have an older sister and a younger brother. My parents grew up in Brooklyn, and we moved out to the island when I was about five. Pretty normal stuff. We've always been a close family and still are today. That's about it. Like I said, not much to tell. Pretty boring stuff."

"Boring is good," replied Violet. "Too much excitement is not good for a family. It overwhelms the important things. A simple life is a blessed life, my mother always says. Do you call your mother often?"

"Yes, ma'am," said Luca. "Every Sunday night, at least. She's very worried about me because we play games on Sundays. She always asks if I went to church. I feel bad, because I have been pretty lazy about it recently. We play a lot of double headers on Saturdays, and I have taken to sleeping late on Sundays since the games usually start at two p.m. Being on the road can really drain you. I guess I need to get back on track with that, as Sammi Jo would say."

"Why don't you join us at church one Sunday?" suggested Violet. "We know that it can be hard to go to a new church where you don't know anyone. At least you'll know us, and we have a very welcoming congregation."

"I'd like that," Luca replied. "I'll call you when I'm going to be around, and we can make arrangements. As long as I can be at the ballpark by one, that is."

Henry winked at Luca and said, "If the preacher goes long, I know how to sneak you out early. Did that a lot when I was young."

As Henry was finishing his comment, Luca stood. Savannah had walked into the room.

Henry followed his gaze. "Well, looks like the princess has arrived."

"I hope my parents didn't grill you too severely," said Savannah.

"Not at all," replied Luca. "We just had a wonderful conversation. Are you ready to go?"

"Yes," said Savannah, "but I need to talk with Mama for a minute. Would you excuse us?" She then motioned for her mama to join her in her bedroom.

When they were behind closed doors, Savannah whispered, "So, Mama, did he pass your test?"

"Yes, dear," replied Violet, "with flying colors. He seems like a nice boy from a good family. He even agreed to come to church with us the next Sunday he is in town."

"Mama!" Savannah exclaimed. "I don't even know if I like him yet. If he comes there with us, what will Jimmy Simmons think?"

"I guess that's a bridge we will cross if it comes to that," said her mama. "You know you can't string two boys along at the same time, don't you, sweetie? As your daddy says, you have to fish or cut bait. Now, go on your date, have a nice time, and we can talk about it when you come home." She kissed Savannah and shooed her out of the bedroom.

Upon entering the living room, they saw Sammi Jo and Pat in the kitchen with Luca and Henry. Sammi Jo was holding her bat and Luca was showing her how to adjust her grip to have a more fluid swing. Sammi Jo was beaming.

"Samantha Jolene!" said Violet, "How many times have I told you not to swing your bat in the house?"

"I wasn't swinging, Mama," replied Sammi Jo, "Luca was just giving me some major league tips."

"Minor league tips," Luca corrected. "I'm not a major leaguer yet."

"But you will be someday, so in my book, that counts," said Sammi Jo. "Mama, he also showed Pat how to throw a circle change! We are going back outside to try it all out."

"Okay," said Violet, "but if you hit another ball through my window, you won't leave your room for a week!"

"Got it, Mama!" Sammi Jo called as she and Pat ran out the door.

As the screen door slammed, Violet heard Pat say, "He is cute!"

"I guess," Sammi Jo replied, "but he has poor taste in girls. Come on, let's get some hitting in before it gets dark."

Violet stood in the doorway and watched her girls. Luca held the door of his car open for Savannah, who giggled and tossed her hair. Sammi Jo paused from digging in for the first pitch from Pat, watching her sister and Luca with a slightly disgusted look on her face. Then she shook her head and adjusted her grip, focusing back on what she was doing. Violet waved as Luca and Savannah drove away, then turned and went back inside.

CHAPTER TWELVE

The day after the first date with Luca, Savannah was insufferable. All she could talk about was what a great time she had, what a wonderful restaurant Luca had chosen to take her to, and what a great listener he was. Sitting on the back porch and listening to Savannah talk with Mama and Daddy in the kitchen through the still-broken kitchen window, Sammi Jo had the image of Savannah running her mouth all night long while Luca suffered in silence, enduring the verbal onslaught and praying for the evening to end. She knew she might just be imagining all of that, but still, that image made her smile.

Sammi Jo wasn't sure what she had been hoping for. Maybe that Luca would somehow put Savannah in her place, or see through her shallow pretense of liking baseball, or even tell her to stop being weird around him. She believed that Luca was too nice to do any of that, but a girl could dream, couldn't she?

She heard Savannah say they had agreed to a second date after Luca got back from the next road trip. This time, Savannah would pick the activity and the place to eat.

You would have thought that Luca had asked her to arrange another invasion of Normandy. Savannah interrogated everyone in the family, including Granny, about what to do and where to go. When she had asked Sammi Jo about her ideas, Sammi Jo had suggested the batting cages and then hot dogs at Shorty's. Savannah was horrified and looked at Sammi Jo as if she had suggested that they attend an execution. That made Sammi Jo laugh out loud.

As the week wore on, Savannah's focus shifted toward church on Sunday and what she would wear to sit with Jimmy Simmons' family. She apparently had no intention of telling him about her date with Luca. That made Sammi Jo mad all over again, although she had no idea why. Why should she care what Savannah did or what the impact would be on two stupid boys who had horrible taste in girls? It was none of her business, right? All of this relationship stuff was confusing.

She decided to go and find Pat and see if she wanted to pitch to her for a while. She gathered up her glove and bat and headed to Pat's house. Her aunt Geraldine told her that Pat was being punished and couldn't go out to play, but she allowed Sammi Jo to go to Pat's room to visit.

Without knocking, Sammi Jo walked into Pat's room. She found her sitting on her bed reading. "Hey Pat, I heard you were being punished; want to talk for a while?" Sammi Jo asked.

"Sure," replied Pat, putting her book aside.

"What are you reading?" asked Sammi Jo.

"A book called *Wuthering Heights*. It's one of the books assigned for summer reading," said Pat.

"What's it about?" Sammi Jo asked.

"Hard to say," Pat responded. "The cover says it's about love, family, revenge, and betrayal, but to me so far, it's mostly about confusion."

"Sounds like my house about now," said Sammi Jo. She went on to tell Pat all about how Savannah had rambled on all week about her date with Luca and how she was going to church on Sunday with Jimmy Simmons and that neither Luca nor Jimmy were aware of the other.

"Don't you think that's kind of crummy?" asked Sammi Jo.

"I don't know," said Pat. "Maybe she hasn't made up her mind who she likes yet and doesn't want to upset anyone until she is sure."

"I think you're giving her too much credit," Sammi Jo replied. "I think she knows exactly what she's doing. Luca is busy all week playing baseball or on the road traveling, and Jimmy Simmons is in town and at church on Sundays. She wants the best of both worlds. She wants to have her cake and eat it, too. It makes me sick."

"Why do you care?" asked Pat. "It doesn't seem like it's any of your business."

That made Sammi Jo stop and think. "I don't know," she replied. "It just doesn't seem right to me. It bothers me that she gets whatever she wants and never seems to suffer any consequences. I, on the other hand, break one window, and I get punished immediately."

"Three windows," reminded Pat. "Two this summer and one last fall. Just saying."

"Regardless," replied Sammi Jo, "it seems that some justice might be in order here."

"What do you mean?" Pat asked. "What do you have up your sleeve?"

"Not sure yet," said Sammi Jo, "but whatever it is, it'll be good."

Sunday came, and once again, Savannah flounced into the kitchen wearing her new buttercup-colored sundress and her new white shoes that her dad bought her.

Sammi Jo commented, "Are you dressed for the Kentucky Derby or church?"

"Be quiet, Sammi Jo," replied Savannah. "It's better than wearing the same clothes every Sunday like you do."

"I go to church for God, not Jimmy Simmons," replied Sammi Jo snarkily.

Savannah spit out the milk she was drinking. "You just better shut up, you little brat. You know nothing about any of this, so just keep your comments to yourself. You have no idea."

"Maybe," said Sammi Jo, "but I'm not blind, and I'm not stupid."

"What does that mean?" asked Savannah.

"Nothing, just saying," said Sammi Jo as she walked out the kitchen door to her father's truck.

All through service, Sammi Jo kept sneaking looks at Savannah sitting with Jimmy Simmons and his family. It was so sickening that she couldn't even focus on her prayers.

"Sammi Jo, turn around. It's rude to keep staring," chided Violet. "Focus on what the pastor is saying and pay attention." She reluctantly dragged her eyes back to the pulpit where the pastor was finishing reading from scripture.

"The biblical account concludes with this passage," said the pastor, " 'Jacob lay with Rachel also, and he loved Rachel more than Leah. And he worked for Laban another seven years.' Genesis 29:30." He put the Bible down and addressed the congregation.

"Yes, this is a story of love, but it is also a story of envy. Jacob loved Rachel more than he loved Leah, the older sister, but Rachel was still envious of her older sister and nothing was ever enough for her.

"We read in the biblical account that Rachel was immature and forever dissatisfied. She took every opportunity to denigrate Leah in Jacob's eyes. Instead of thanking God for her relationship with Jacob, she had to have more. She had to catch up with her sister. That's a classic symptom of envy—it is insatiable. How do you think Leah felt? No matter how many children she had, Jacob would never love her as much as he loved Rachel. Meanwhile, Rachel could have been gracious and generous to her unloved older sister, but she wasn't. We don't read of her doing a single kind, unselfish act. You all know the rest of the story. What havoc jealousy and envy wrought upon this family!

"Are those same destructive emotions of jealousy and envy evident in you? In case you aren't aware of the symptoms of jealousy and envy, give yourself this test. Ask yourself, do you examine others with a critical eye? Do you have hidden feelings of inferiority? Do you complain about not getting fair treatment? Do you need a lot of recognition for your achievements? Do you find it hard to pay compliments to others? Do you keep score of your own good deeds and those of others? Are you willing to pass along negative rumors about a successful person?

"If you answered yes to some of these questions, you may be having trouble with envy, even though you haven't recognized it."

The pastor then stepped from the pulpit, said the final blessing, and dismissed the congregation. On the way out of church, Sammi Jo caught Pat's eye as she was exiting her pew. She mouthed for her to wait up and Pat waited. When Sammi Jo got to where she was, they began walking out of the church together.

"Do you remember what we talked about?" asked Sammi Jo.

"Sure," replied Pat. "But are you sure you want to go forward with it after what the pastor just said?"

"Yeah," replied Sammi Jo. "This isn't about jealousy or

envy; it's about justice. Someone has to stop this, and I am going to do it. Come on before they get too far ahead."

The cousins made their way through the crowd and spotted Savannah and Jimmy standing together by his new truck. Jimmy had recently enlisted in the Marines and would be leaving in a few weeks for Parris Island, South Carolina. The whole town had been talking about it and how Jimmy had just bought a new truck with the signing bonus he received. As he was proudly showing the truck to Savannah, the two cousins arrived.

"Hey, Jimmy!" said Sammi Jo. "Nice truck."

"Thanks, kid," Jimmy replied. "I was just telling your sister that it's the first new truck the family has ever had. I can hardly believe it."

Sammi Jo looked at Savannah. She had a look of terror on her face as Sammi Jo turned to look at Pat, waiting for her scripted question.

Pat looked at Jimmy and asked. "When do you leave for boot camp?"

"At the end of the summer," replied Jimmy. "Why do you ask?"

Sammi Jo jumped right into the opening, "We were just talking about how maybe we should all go have some fun together before you leave. After all, you have this great new truck we can all fit into, and I'm sure Savannah wouldn't mind." Sammi Jo shot Savannah a snarky look before continuing.

Savannah's look of terror had now turned to sadness as she recognized what her sister had planned. All of a sudden, Sammi Jo saw the same sad eyes that the pastor had described Jacob's wife Leah as having, and a tear on Savannah's cheek. She hesitated. She could not take her eyes off of her older sister, who seemed to be silently begging her not to do this. She tore her eyes away from

Savannah and addressed Jimmy.

"Maybe we can go to a movie. I hear that the new Rocky movie is playing at the drive-in for the next few weeks, maybe we can see that together?" Pat just stared at Sammi Jo with her mouth open.

"That sounds like fun," replied Jimmy. "Savannah, would you be okay with that?"

Savannah replied quietly, looking at her sister, "Sure, that sounds okay to me."

Pat grabbed Sammi Jo by the elbow and said to Jimmy, "Well, we have to go. Congratulations on the new truck!" As she dragged Sammi Jo out of earshot, she asked her, "What happened? You were supposed to ask him to take us to a Bulls game."

"I know," replied Sammi Jo, "but I couldn't do it. They looked so happy before we got there, and I don't know, maybe I don't care as much as I thought."

"Well, I'm glad," said Pat. "Savannah would have been so mad at us, and we don't need that kind of stress this summer. We only have a month left, so let's enjoy it."

Sammi Jo put her arm around Pat and said, "Sounds good to me. Want to go fishing when we get home?"

CHAPTER THIRTEEN

The rest of the summer flew by for Sammi Jo. They had a blast at the drive-in with Savannah and Jimmy, and Savannah seemed more relaxed and fun than Sammi Jo could ever recall. Sammi Jo was also beginning to realize what a genuinely nice and funny guy Jimmy was. She felt bad that she had ever thought about hurting him and Savannah, and as the summer wore on, she sensed that the wall that had been built between her and her sister was starting to crumble.

Savannah and Luca had continued to date when he was in town, and Sammi Jo found that it didn't bother her as much as it had. Without the anger, she found that she was really able to enjoy talking with Luca even when Savannah was around. What's more, Savannah was okay when Sammi Jo asked Luca to pitch to her in the backyard one evening before they went on a date. That had been a great time, and Sammi Jo thought about that for days afterward.

The only drama was when Mama had invited Luca to church for homecoming after his road trip to play the Kinston Eagles. Jimmy had not yet left for boot camp, and that threw Savannah into a significant state of distress. Everything was resolved when Savannah started throwing up on Sunday morning and Mama told her she had to stay home. Sammi Jo could never quite figure out how Savannah had contrived that miracle, but it didn't matter. She got to sit next to Luca through the whole service, and it was the best church service she had ever attended. She loved introducing Luca to the other kids at the homecoming celebration afterward and telling them that he was going to be in the major leagues someday because she had helped him with his swing. That was a *great* day.

The end of the summer was bad for Savannah. Jimmy left for boot camp the last week of August. Luca was set to leave for home on September 2nd after the playoffs, which the Bulls had lost in a close series against the Winston-Salem Red Sox. Luca had a fantastic series and was confident that the Braves AA affiliate was looking at him for next year. This was great for Luca, not so good for Savannah.

Before leaving, Luca visited the family to thank everyone for their friendship and hospitality. He softened the blow of his departure a bit by giving Savannah a very pretty and simple white gold charm bracelet with a single baseball charm on it. She seemed genuinely touched by the unexpected gift, and they both promised to stay in touch and see each other as soon as it was convenient for both of them.

Luca also surprised Sammi Jo with a gift. After he gave the charm bracelet to Savannah, he excused himself and went back out to the porch. He returned carrying a big box and a bag. He strode over to where Sammi Jo was sitting next to her dad and handed her the box.

"For me?" Sammi Jo asked, genuinely surprised.

"Sure," said Luca, "how could I forget to thank my favorite batting coach? You seriously saved my season. This is just my way of saying thank you with a gift that will always remind you of me. Open it!"

Sammi Jo tore open the box, and out jumped the cutest little puppy she had ever seen. He immediately began licking her and then promptly peed on her due to the excitement.

"Sorry about that, Mrs. Jackson," said Luca to Violet. "I guess I had him in the box too long. I checked with Henry before bringing the pup over here, he said it would be okay."

Before Violet could reply Sammi Jo asked, "Where did you get him? He's perfect!"

"When I got back from the last playoff game in Winston-Salem," began Luca, "I was the last one out of the locker room. As I was walking under the stands out to my car, I heard something whimpering. I followed the sound, and there under the first row of seats along the first base line, I saw a puppy. The mother must have died or gotten killed before she could return to him. It was pitiful. He was hungry and was scavenging for popcorn that had fallen through the stands. So, I grabbed him and wrapped him in my coat and brought him home. I've been caring for him all week, and he has really responded. I thought that he would make a great companion for you because he apparently loves baseball and popcorn, too! Born right there at El Toro Park."

"Why don't you young people take him outside so he can run around and get used to his environment?" suggested Violet.

Sammi Jo was up and out of her seat before her mama finished her sentence. Savannah and Luca followed, and soon they were all playing with and enjoying the new addition to the family.

"What's his name?" asked Sammi Jo as the puppy took a break to relieve himself again.

"I named him Casey," replied Luca.

"Why Casey?" asked Sammi Jo.

"Let me show you why," said Luca as he reached into the bag he was still holding and pulled out a book. "Remember how I mentioned a few weeks back how I love to read and write poetry? Well, I thought that you might like this book." He handed it to her as Savannah looked over his shoulder.

Sammi Jo read the cover out loud. *"Casey at the Bat and other Timeless Baseball Poems."*

" 'Casey at the Bat' was one of the classic poems my dad would read to me, my brother, and sister," said Luca. "It was probably the one poem that really started my love of poetry. I've really studied poetry in depth since then, and in college, I majored in literature. I always assumed I would be playing baseball professionally, so I just studied what really interested me. We even examined 'Casey at the Bat' in one of my poetry classes. The professor said it was actually one of the classic poems of all time because it combined incredibly descriptive writing with baseball, which is very hard to do well. My two loves in one, what could be better! I thought you might enjoy it, too, since I know how much you love the game."

Sammi Jo didn't know what to say. Savannah jumped in to help her out. "How sweet, Luca, what a great idea. Sammi Jo enjoys reading and loves baseball. That's such a perfect and thoughtful gift." She gave Luca a soft kiss on the cheek.

"Yes, it is," agreed Sammi Jo, finally finding her voice. "Thank you. I will read every page." She approached Luca, gave him a huge hug, then ran off to catch up with Casey, who was now grappling with her baseball glove.

"I have a book for you, too, Savannah," said Luca, reaching into the bag again. He pulled out a small book and handed it to her. The cover said *The Love Poems of Lord*

Byron.

Savannah looked at Luca and said, "This is lovely. I have never read real poetry before, but I'm definitely going to start."

"Wonderful," replied Luca as he took her hand. "I want you to start on page forty-eight, with the poem 'She Walks in Beauty'. It reminds me so much of you, and when you read it, I'm hoping you will see why. I know we haven't known each other long and haven't spent as much time together this summer as I hoped, but I have grown very fond of you, Savannah. I'm hoping that this is not the end for us. If the Savannah Braves don't pick up my contract for the 1981 season, I'll be back here with the Bulls. If they do, then I'll be playing in a city with your name, so how could I forget you? Either way, please write to me. I want to know everything you're doing. Okay?"

Savannah was starting to cry, which confused Luca. "I don't want to put any pressure on you, Savannah, please don't cry. We can do this at your own pace. I just wanted you to know how I felt before I left."

"It's not that," said Savannah. "It's just that I am fond of you, too, and no one has ever been this sweet to me before. I don't see how I can measure up to your image of me. I'm just a regular country girl, not someone who guys write poems about."

"That is one of the things I find so sweet and innocent about you. You are completely unaware of how lovely you are," said Luca as he looked into her eyes. "You are stronger than you know and more beautiful than you realize. Just take whatever time you need to figure this out. I'll wait for you. All I ask is that you do what your heart tells you to do. Whatever you decide, I will be okay, I promise."

Sammi Jo was watching them as she played with Casey.

They were holding hands and talking. Savannah seemed to be upset by something Luca said and was crying. Then she saw Savannah nod her head and they hugged tight for a long time. Sammi Jo looked away, slightly embarrassed to have eavesdropped on their private moment. She found a baseball and threw it for Casey to chase. He darted off after it and pounced on it.

It was too big for him, so he just poked at it with his nose and barked. She thought to herself, yeah, little Casey, it's too big for you now, but someday, that baseball will be just the right size, and then what fun you are going to have!

CHAPTER FOURTEEN

———————◇———————

Fall 1980

As soon as Luca left for home, Sammi Jo felt that change was in the air. School was starting again in less than a week and fall was fast approaching. All of this made her remember her promise to God that if He would let her stay the way she was until the end of baseball season, she would try to change to be more like Savannah and stop being so immature. This past summer had been a real learning experience for her, and she felt more confident than ever that she could do anything she put her mind to.

As she sat on her bed with Casey, she finally opened the book Luca gave her a few days ago. She immediately opened to "Casey at the Bat" and began to read out loud so her puppy could listen.

The outlook wasn't brilliant for the Mudville Nine that day:
The score stood four to two, with but one inning more to play,
And then when Cooney died at first, and Barrows did the same,
A pall-like silence fell upon the patrons of the game.

By the end of that first stanza, she was hooked. She read the whole poem and then reread it two more times. Finally, she put the book down and said to Casey, "Wow, that was some story! It's just like Daddy said, it's never over until the final strike. Everything comes down to that. Remember that, Casey, always."

She put down the book and promised herself to read more later before bed. Right now, she had to begin the change that she was determined to make in herself. As she stood in front of her closet deciding what she would wear for the first week of her junior year at Wake Forest High School, she had a moment of weakness.

"There is no way I can wear what the other girls wear *every* day. Maybe there's some halfway measure. Maybe I can change slowly over time." She started to pick out clothes with that thought in mind. She took out a dress for the first day, jeans for the second day, and a skirt for the third day. After she had her first week of clothes laid out on the bed, she changed her mind. "No, I have to be all in from the start," she told herself. "No halfway measures! Swing for the fences right from the first pitch."

She put everything back and started over again. This time she laid out all of the new clothes that her mama had bought for her earlier in the summer. She was worried when she saw how few outfits she really had and that she only had two pairs of shoes to go with it all. She started to panic. She really was unprepared for the magnitude of the change she was trying to make all at once. Then she had the most terrifying thought.

"Oh my goodness! I forgot about makeup! I have none, and I have no idea how to put it on!" Overwhelmed, she fell face first on the bed and began to weep. Casey came and nuzzled her, trying to console her, but it was no use.

Suddenly, there was a knock on the door. "Are you okay in there, Sammi Jo? Is something wrong?" Savannah inquired.

"I'm okay," replied Sammi Jo, trying to compose

herself.

"May I come in?" asked Savannah.

"Sure," replied Sammi Jo, standing and wiping her eyes.

Savannah entered the bedroom, saw the pile of clothes and shoes, and asked, "What are you doing and why are you crying?"

Sammi Jo broke down again and couldn't explain. Savannah surveyed the room and understood. "You're trying to figure out what to wear for the first week of school, aren't you?" Sammi Jo nodded.

"Then why are all your Sunday clothes out on the bed?" Savannah put her arms around Sammi Jo as she continued to sob, unable to answer her sister's question. As Savannah stood there holding her sobbing sister, it all became clear.

She held Sammi Jo out at arm's length. "You're going to start dressing up for school, aren't you?" Again, Sammi Jo just nodded. "And you have no idea how to do it, do you?" asked Savannah. "Do you want my help?" Sammi Jo started sobbing even harder and nodded her head vigorously.

"Oh, you poor girl," said Savannah, holding her sister close. "Of course I'll help you! Come on, let's do this right now." As she started to sort through the pile of possibilities on Sammi Jo's bed, she suddenly stopped and said, "I have a better idea. Before we dig into this pile, let's go shopping."

Sammi Jo looked at her like she was crazy, since they had recently shopped with Mama and had bought more clothes than they had budgeted for. There was no way their parents were going to let them spend more money on clothes right now.

"Where?" asked Sammi Jo. "And how? We can't spend any more money on clothes after what Daddy just paid for."

"I know a place that has *lots* of clothes that will be perfect and won't cost a thing," replied Savannah.

"Where is that?" asked Sammi Jo, wiping at her tears.

Savannah put her arm around her sister. "Come with me, little sister, we are going shopping at a quaint little place called Savannah's Closet."

They spent the rest of the afternoon pulling clothes out of Savannah's closet and having Sammi Jo try them on. To their surprise, most of the clothes fit reasonably well. Even some of Savannah's shoes worked for Sammi Jo.

By the end of the afternoon, they had identified enough clothes that, when combined with Sammi Jo's own collection, gave Sammi Jo new outfits for a month.

They hung them in Sammi Jo's closet in the order she would wear them to make it easier for her. The shoes were lined up underneath the matching outfits.

As they sat on the bed resting, they surveyed the fruit of their combined efforts. "Well," said Savannah, "that was fun. Are you feeling better about all this, Sammi Jo? Are you ready for the new you?"

Sammi Jo leaned into her sister, putting her head on her shoulder, "Yeah, but part of me wishes I didn't have to."

"What does the other part say?" asked Savannah.

"The other part knows it's time." said Sammi Jo. "I need to do this. Not just for Mama or Daddy, or even you. I need to do it for me. I just wonder who I'll be when I'm done."

Savannah put her arm around her sister and said, "Seriously? Just because you're trying to transform yourself doesn't mean that you will become someone else! You will still be you, but with improvements. Trust me, if I thought all of this would change you into someone you're not, I would be the first one to stop you. I love you just as you are, and so do Mama and Daddy."

"Are you sure?" asked Sammi Jo.

"Absolutely," Savannah replied, "and I will be there for you the whole way. Just let me help."

"Can you help me with makeup?" asked Sammi Jo with a quiver in her voice. "That stuff scares me even more than the clothes."

Taking her sister's face in her hands and looking at it closely Savannah said. "Now *that* might be a challenge!" Then, winking and smiling, she added, "But I'm practically a professional, and I have quite a few tricks up my sleeve. Let's work on that tomorrow. Tonight, let's just have dinner and spend some time with Casey. I think he needs some attention."

Sammi Jo hugged her older sister tightly. "Thank you. I don't know what I would do without you." Then, she picked up Casey, and they walked into the kitchen where dinner was waiting.

When the semester started, Sammi Jo felt like she was attending a different school. From the first day, the girls seemed friendlier and the boys weirder. She had been invited to a few "new school year" parties, but she didn't feel comfortable accepting yet. She had never been a shrinking violet or even close to being described as introverted, but this year, she was feeling her way through every situation with caution. She wasn't being as proactive in her conversations and had taken to waiting for people to speak with her before responding. When that happened, she became more like herself, and would speak freely.

She had gone to school for years with these same people, but now she was seeing them all in a different light, through different eyes; especially Bobby Curtis.

When he spoke to her in history class on the first day of school, her heart literally stopped for a few seconds. He had never spoken to her before, *ever*, and when he did, she was so stunned that when her heart started beating again, she could only smile and nod. He actually seemed to like that and continued the conversation all by himself for five more minutes.

From what Sammi Jo could remember of that first interaction, he had asked her if she was a football fan and if she was going to the first home game of the year that Friday night. She just nodded and smiled, and Bobby took that as confirmation that she would be there specifically to watch him play.

She remembered that he said that he was going to be the starting quarterback and was confident that the team would dominate the league. Sammi Jo remembered all of that but nothing of the history lesson that day. When she got home, she asked her father to tell her everything he knew about the game of football, what a quarterback did, and how they scored.

The weekend came and Sammi Jo was there on Friday night with the rest of the student body and fans. She had asked Pat to go with her, and Pat, who was in the grade behind her at Wake Forest High, was thrilled to go. They found seats high in the stands far from anyone else so they could concentrate on the game and talk without being overheard.

"Can you believe that Bobby Curtis asked me if I was coming?" asked Sammi Jo. "He hasn't said two words to me since we started school together. Why now?"

"I don't know," said Pat munching on some pretzels she had purchased at the concession stand. "Maybe it was just time?"

"What do you mean?" asked Sammi Jo. "Time for

what?"

"You know," said Pat, "people, even boys, know when it is time to break out. To finally get the courage to talk to someone you've liked for years but didn't have the courage to speak to before. The beginning of a school year is one of those times, filled with all sorts of new opportunities and new starts. Maybe this is a new start for Bobby. Maybe you, too," she said as she took a sip of her Coke.

"So, you think he likes me? Is that why he asked me if I was going?" said Sammi Jo.

"Could be," said Pat, "but don't assume anything. Just make sure he knows you were here and try to remember a specific play or two where he really does well. Mention those to him and then leave it at that. Make him come after you, boys really like that."

They spent the rest of the game laser focused on Bobby, and between them, they recorded the specifics of a few of Bobby's highlights in the program. He had a lot of them, so they just circled the two or three that had made the crowd cheer the loudest. Those were the ones that Sammi Jo wanted to remember.

Things had gone well the next week at school. Bobby spoke to her again in history class, and she was successful in recalling the highlights she had memorized. Bobby seemed very impressed and pleased, but they didn't speak again until Thursday. Sammi Jo thought that maybe Bobby had just been being nice and had lost interest.

When he approached her in the cafeteria on Thursday, she pretended not to see him coming. He sat next to her at the table, but she kept her back to him and continued to seem engaged in conversation with the girls at her table.

After a few minutes, he tapped her on the shoulder and said, "Excuse me, Sammi Jo, can I speak with you for a moment?"

She turned to him and gave him a big smile. "Sure, what's up?"

"We have an away game this Friday night," Bobby started, "but on Saturday, a few of us are getting together at Steve Holden's house, would you like to go?"

"Can I get back with you on that?" asked Sammi Jo, startled by the sudden invitation. "I have to check my calendar. Give me your phone number, and I'll call you Saturday if I can go. What time is the party?"

They discussed the details, Sammi Jo wrote it all down, and after Bobby left, she excused herself from the table, went to the girls' room, and threw up.

Friday night was filled with consultations with her mama, Savannah, and Pat. It was decided that she should go but should tell him that she could only stay for an hour. That would give her time to find out if she were comfortable and then have a ready excuse to leave if she were not. They also identified the proper clothes for a Saturday night get together. Something very pretty but comfortable, like nice jeans and a pretty top. They also told her to let him do most of the talking and to ask him a lot of questions about himself.

She called his house the next day and left a message with his mom that she could attend for an hour and would meet him there. After hanging up, Sammi Jo shook for the next five minutes, unsure if it was from adrenaline or terror. She thought to herself, this self-improvement program is really getting scary.

"Mama, do you really think I can do this?" Sammi Jo asked as she sat in the truck with her mother outside of Steve Holden's house. "I feel like I want to go back home."

"You're just nervous, honey," replied Violet. "We all get nervous in unfamiliar situations. That never goes away, but it does get easier to deal with over time. Don't make too much of a big deal about this. I'm sure there will be other girls there, and you only have to stay for an hour. If things get uncomfortable with Bobby, just excuse yourself, go to the restroom and then just go talk with the other girls for a while. I'll be back here in an hour. Okay?"

"Promise?" asked Sammi Jo.

"Promise," her mama replied. "All you're doing here is stepping into the box and taking a few swings. What's so scary about that? Think about it like that. You've done that a million times. Just keep swinging."

"Got it, Mama," said Sammi Jo. "I can do that." She gave her mama a kiss, got out, and walked into the batter's box.

The evening was a whirl of hellos, hugs, and music. Bobby had met her as soon as she came through the door and introduced her to everyone there. She recognized most of them but had never been really friendly with any of them before. She spent a few minutes catching up with a few of the girls, and when Bobby came back with some punch for her, they found a quiet corner and sat.

They talked about the game on Friday night and about Bobby's exploits that helped the team win. He was so excited and animated that it made Sammi Jo relax. She didn't have to carry the conversation, and that really helped. She found herself laughing, a lot.

Before she knew it, her hour was up. She knew her mama would be outside waiting for her, and she wasn't sure what to do. All she could hear was Pat's voice in her head telling her to make him come after her. She thought about her mother's baseball analogy and thought, well this "at bat" seemed to go well. I've made it to first base and maybe that's enough for this inning. I don't want to get tagged out trying to stretch a single into a double.

She stood from the couch. "I'm sorry, Bobby," she said,

"but I have to go. I had a great time, thanks for inviting me. Will you walk me to the door?"

Bobby looked genuinely disappointed but agreed. When they got to the door, Bobby asked if she would be coming to the home game next Friday night. She said she would and that she hoped to see him at school next week. Bobby smiled that huge, electric smile of his and gave her a gentle hug.

"Great," he said. "You just made my night."

Sammi Jo didn't remember walking to the car or even opening the door.

Violet asked her, "So, how did it go, sweetie?"

"Great, Mama," she replied. "I think I got a hit and am on first base."

CHAPTER FIFTEEN

———◇———

Luca called once a week to speak with Savannah. This time, he called and also asked to speak with Sammi Jo.

"Really?" she asked Savannah, who was handing her the phone. "He wants to speak with me?"

"Yes, but make it quick, it's expensive," Savannah replied. As Sammi Jo took the phone from her, she got butterflies in her stomach.

"Hey Luca, it's Sammi Jo. What's up?"

"Not too much, slugger," Luca replied. "I just wanted to find out how school is going for you. Junior year can be fun but sometimes tough. Everything going okay?"

"Yeah," replied Sammi Jo, "everything is great. I've made a few changes, and it has really made a difference."

"What kind of changes and what kind of difference?" asked Luca.

"Well," Sammi Jo hedged, then decided to open up, "I'm dating someone. He's the quarterback on the football team, and he's really nice."

There was silence on the phone for a minute as Luca absorbed the news. "A boyfriend? Well, that certainly is a change. Have your parents met him? Does he also play baseball?"

Sammi Jo laughed at the last question. "My parents

have known his parents forever, and we've gone to school together for years. And no, unfortunately, he does not like baseball. He is all about football and thinks baseball is too slow and boring. I'm hoping that I can change his mind about that over time."

"Over time?" asked Luca. "So, you're thinking this is going to last, huh?"

"I don't know," replied Sammi Jo. "I'm just going to see how it goes, learn about how all this relationship stuff works. I'm just a rookie, you know."

Luca laughed, "Just go slow and take your time. You're a very sweet girl, and the guy who ends up with you is going to be very lucky. Make him earn it, understand? *And*, I don't trust anyone who doesn't like baseball."

Not really understanding, but getting that he was being complimentary, Sammi Jo replied, "I will, Luca. Thanks for talking with me. I'll put Savannah back on. See ya!"

She handed Savannah the phone and went to her room. She saw the book of baseball poetry on her bed and went back out to the kitchen. She tapped Savannah on the shoulder and whispered, "Tell him I read 'Casey at the Bat' and loved it. Tell him to send me more poems to read."

Looking annoyed by the interruption, Savannah returned to her conversation. "By the way, Luca, Sammi Jo said she read the 'Casey and the Bat' story and really liked it. She said you should send her more poems to read."

Luca responded, " '*At* the Bat'. It's 'Casey *at* the Bat', and it's a poem, not a story."

"Whatever," replied Savannah. "Either way, she liked it."

"Tell her I'll send her some more to read soon," Luca said.

Luca called many times over the following months, and each time, he also asked to speak with Sammi Jo. He had

79

sent her poems to read which he had written and others that were just his favorites. Sammi Jo read them all and loved every one. Especially the ones Luca wrote.

Some were about baseball, but most were about other things, like life, family, and love. She began to find every book she could about writing and reading poetry and found it all so fascinating.

She wrote back to him with a few of her first attempts at poetry. She knew they weren't great, but Luca always said he liked them and really encouraged her to just keep writing. He said it was like hitting, that you needed a lot of batting practice before you found the perfect swing. She liked that analogy and took it to heart. She picked up the *Casey at the Bat* book where she kept all of the letters and poems that he had sent her. Taking out a couple of her favorites, she unfolded her favorite one so far. It was titled, "The Angel's Gift".

> *To fall in love*
> *To be in love*
> *To be sure of love*
> *To know love and to have love know you*
> *To have the one you love be in love with you*

She didn't know if she understood it all, but she knew in her heart it was true. To someday have all of those things would certainly be a gift from heaven. That she could understand.

Savannah was also getting letters from Jimmy Simmons. While at boot camp, he had not been allowed to call, but he could write letters. He told Savannah that he had another five weeks of boot camp and that she could visit him with his parents when they came for graduation. That did not make Savannah happy. She was hoping she could visit with him much sooner than that. With Luca up north and Jimmy at Parris Island, she was getting pretty tired of just working and hanging out at home.

On one of those many nights at home, Savannah took out the book of poems that Luca had given her and started to read. She had made many other attempts to get through them but could not. She struggled with the old-time phrases and tempo and got lost in the phrasing. She felt like she was reading a completely different language. But tonight, she was determined to understand. She opened to page forty-eight and once again started to read, "She Walks in Beauty".

She walks in beauty, like the night

Okay, she thought to herself, I kind of get that. The night can certainly be beautiful. But how does the night walk? She moved to the next line.

Of cloudless climes and starry skies;

She wondered, what is a cloudless clime? I know what starry skies are, that's easy. I'll just forget about the climes and focus on the stars.

That was when Sammi Jo came in and sat on the couch beside her.

"Whatcha doin'?" she asked Savannah.

"Just trying to get through the poem that Luca told me to read," she replied. "He said it reminded him of me, but I can't even get through the first few lines without getting confused."

"Want some help?" asked Sammi Jo sliding closer to her sister to get a look at the poem. "I've been doing a lot of reading about how to write and read poetry since Luca gave me my book. I've even tried writing some of my own. Maybe I can figure it out. Do you want me to try?"

Savannah handed her the book and said, "Yes. I'm so embarrassed every time Luca asks me if I've read it and I have to tell him no and make some excuse. I'm sure I've hurt his feelings. I need to know if this is something good or bad that he is comparing me to. Maybe if you read it to me, I'll understand it better."

Sammi Jo scanned the poem, reading it silently to herself, and smiled. "First of all," she said, "it is a very good thing that he compared you to. Second, I think I see why you were having a tough time. Let me read it, and you'll see."

She began to read it as the author intended it to be read.

She walks in beauty, like the night
Of cloudless climes and starry skies;
And all that's best of dark and bright
Meet in her aspect and her eyes.

"Do you see?" Sammi Jo said. "You were probably reading each line separately; they are supposed to be read together. They flow together and create a continual statement. Understand?"

Savannah was starting to smile. "I think so. It made so much more sense when you read it, but I still don't know what a clime is or what aspect means."

"I know," replied Sammi Jo, "some of the old phrases are tough. I've struggled with a bunch of them myself, so I just look them up."

Sammi Jo went to her room and got the dictionary that

she used to look up words that she didn't understand. When she returned, she sat down next to Savannah and opened to the entry for clime.

"Clime refers in general to the climate of an area or the weather." Then she flipped to the entry for the word aspect. "Aspect means a feature, like the features of your face. So what Lord Byron was doing was comparing some girl to the night and saying that she moves through life beautifully and calmly, like a starry, cloudless night. All that is great and beautiful about a night like that reminds him of her. When he looks in her eyes, that is what he sees."

"Wow," said Savannah, "you got all of that from just those lines? That's amazing. It's like he painted a picture with words. When you read it correctly, I could actually see it in my mind."

"Yes!" exclaimed Sammi Jo. "That's exactly what all the books say poetry is about. Painting with words. Creating worlds with phrases. You get it. You understand!"

Savannah was beaming now. "Read more," she requested, snuggling up closer to Sammi Jo. "I want to know what else he says about me."

Sammi Jo raised an eyebrow. "It's not about you, remember, it's a poem that Luca said reminds him of you. Don't get crazy."

Together, the sisters spent the evening reading the lines and analyzing the meaning. They had fun looking up words or phrases they didn't understand. By the time they were done, Savannah had been reduced to tears at the thought that Luca, or anyone for that matter, could see her in this way. It made her happy but scared her at the same time.

"Sammi Jo," said Savannah, "this is heavy stuff. If I take this the way Luca may have meant it, that may mean I have to break his heart."

"Why?" asked Sammi Jo. "I don't understand. He's so

sweet and cute, and he obviously thinks you 'walk in beauty', as twisted as that may be," she said with a nudge. "What's the problem?"

"The problem is," said Savannah, looking down at her hands, "that I don't miss him as much as I miss Jimmy. I mean, I like talking to him when he calls, but when I'm talking with him, I'm not wishing he were here. When I read Jimmy's letters, the whole time I'm wishing he was here with me sitting on the couch. I'm not upset because Luca hasn't visited, but I am so angry that I can't visit Jimmy for another five weeks."

"Wow," replied Sammi Jo. "That's rough, but I think it's pretty clear. I think you need to tell Luca this. He needs to know."

"I could have before!" exclaimed Savannah. "But now, after reading this poem, how can I do that? Now that I know what he meant by making me read it, I can't do it to him."

"So what are you going to do, pretend that you don't know?" asked Sammi Jo. "String him along and then still break his heart down the road? I've heard it only gets worse the longer you wait. If you really care anything for him, then you need to tell him the truth."

"You really think so?" asked Savannah. "Do you think he'll hate me? Will you hate me? I know how much you like him."

"He will be fine," said Sammi Jo. "He'll probably write a few horrid poems about you, a few 'loved and lost' sonnets, and be done with it. I'm sure he has his own way of working through this kind of thing. He's a tough guy; he can take a loss. Give him some credit."

"In my heart, I know you are right," agreed Savannah. "I never really understood how much I liked Jimmy while he was here, but with him gone, I finally realized it. I know

I have to tell Luca, but it'll be hard. Do you think I can wait until he calls again next week, or do I have to call him now?"

Sammi Jo moved closer to her sister and put her arm around her, "Just wait until he calls. Give yourself some time to work through what you want to say. Just be straight with him, that's all anyone would want—the truth."

The sisters sat there the rest of the night reading through the love poems of Lord Byron, seeing his beautiful word paintings in their heads and becoming closer than they had ever been.

CHAPTER SIXTEEN

It had been five weeks since Savannah broke up with Luca, and she was now on her way to visit Jimmy at Parris Island. She and Jimmy's parents were heading there for graduation week, and Savannah was walking on air. She had told Sammi Jo earlier in the week that breaking it off with Luca felt like a weight had been lifted off of her. It wasn't that she disliked Luca or that she was happy to never see him again, it was just that she didn't have the burden of keeping secrets.

She had decided to come completely clean with Luca. She had told him about Jimmy and how she felt when she read "She Walks in Beauty". Luca had been surprised to learn about Jimmy but seemed to take it all well, at least while he was on the phone with Savannah. He actually thanked her for being truthful and said that it was understandable that she had a hometown relationship with someone that had more in common with her.

He was so understanding and gallant about it all that when Savannah hung up, she didn't even cry, which, to Sammi Jo, was a miracle. Luca had made Savannah believe that she had done the right thing, and that he was happy for her. Sammi Jo suspected that was not the whole story. It seemed too easy.

A few weeks later, a letter arrived from Luca.

"Sammi Jo!" called Violet from the kitchen as she walked in from gathering the mail. "There's a letter for you from Luca. Come out here and get it please."

Sammi Jo was shocked to receive a letter from Luca weeks after the breakup. She had assumed that the whole family's relationship with Luca had also ended. She had not written to Luca since his conversation with Savannah, and it had been five weeks with nothing from him. She took the letter from her mama and went to her room to read it. She plopped down on her bed and opened it.

Hey Slugger,

Sorry I haven't written sooner, but I had some things to think through. Savannah told me that you were a huge part of helping her understand the poem I asked her to read. Thank you for doing that. It obviously opened her eyes and helped her see some things more clearly, and that was a very good thing.

What impressed me most was the initiative you took to dive into the research about poetry and how fast you've learned. You're really getting good. I read the last two poems that you sent, and I can really see development. Keep at it!

I wanted you to know that regardless of the breakup with Savannah, I enjoy our correspondence and would like to stay in touch. You are such a bright light, Sammi Jo, with such a generous spirit. I am looking forward to seeing that reflected in your writing.

I could use some inspiration right now. I still haven't heard from the Savannah Braves, so it looks like I may be back in Durham next summer.

Nothing is certain yet, but the upside is that if I am with the Bulls next season, I get to see you and your parents again. That and the fact that I will have my favorite batting coach close at hand. Either way, let's stay in touch. I look forward to hearing more about "Football Boy", how school is going, and to reading more of your poems. I have included a couple more of my own for your evaluation and comment. Maybe you can be my poetry coach, too?

Keep swinging,
Luca

Sammi Jo was smiling as she put the letter down and opened up the two poems that Luca had included with his letter. She thought to herself, he doesn't sound too upset about it all, I guess he really is as tough as I thought. She opened the first poem and started to read; it was titled "Night Walking."

Walking at night can be beautiful
But be careful where you stride
The dim light is deceiving
For there, some pitfalls hide

Sometimes the stars so far above
Shine light too dim to show
The yawning chasm of deep despair
Lying far below

Sammi Jo thought about what she had just read. He seemed to be referencing the Lord Byron poem that she had read with Savannah. It has some of the same imagery and evoked similar emotions, but this one was sad. This one was about heartbreak. Maybe Luca really did love Savannah, or at least was walking in that direction. Then again, this might have nothing to do with Savannah. Maybe it was about being in the dark about next season. She would have to think about it more.

She put the poem down and opened the next one, titled "The Mustard Seed."

It starts as seed, planted with hope
It's watered with tears of despair
Strengthened with courage from deep in your heart
And nurtured with confident care

With patience and faith it grows day by day
Till one day its golden fruit gleams
And then you can stand on once barren land
And harvest your own field of dreams.

Sammi Jo stared at the poem with awe. Luca was so good at packing his verses with vivid imagery that Sammi Jo could see and feel everything he was describing. The mustard seed, she knew, was from the parable that Jesus told about faith. Luca had used that image to describe the rise from despair to hope. Again she wondered, was this describing his own feelings after the breakup or was it just encouragement? To her, it felt like he was talking about rebuilding after a loss. Turning a barren place into a field of dreams. She could relate to that. That was what she was doing in her own life.

As she folded up the poems, put them with the letter, and gently placed them in her *Casey at the Bat* book with the others, she thought, wow, Luca is even more interesting than I knew. He is really deep and talented in so many ways. I certainly have a lot to learn about writing, life, and Luca.

Especially Luca.

CHAPTER SEVENTEEN

———◇———

Winter 1981

When Savannah returned from her visit with Jimmy at Marine Corps boot camp graduation, she was walking on air. She couldn't stop talking about how much Jimmy had changed, but in a good way. He was still funny and caring, but he seemed so much more mature now. He had always been respectful to his parents, but now that same level of respect also encompassed Savannah. It was as if boot camp had polished his best qualities while softening the worst.

"Then, Mama," said Savannah as she told her story breathlessly, "he told his parents and me that he didn't know where he was going to be stationed next, but that wherever it was, he wanted me near him. He told all of us that the time away from home made him realize how much he loved me and wanted to spend his life with me! Can you believe it?"

"So, are you actually engaged?" asked Violet.

"No," replied Savannah, "not yet. Jimmy was entitled to a ten day leave after graduation but decided to go right into his required marine combat training at Camp Geiger, seventeen miles from Camp Lejeune. That way, he can save his ten days for when we get engaged. He'll be at Camp Geiger for sixty days, and as soon as that's finished, he'll pick his military occupational specialty, and then will know where he'll be stationed. Isn't this so exciting?"

"It is exciting, honey," said Henry, "but what does that mean for you? What are your plans?"

"I think it's pretty clear, Daddy," replied Savannah. "As soon as he finishes MCT, he'll take ten days of leave, come home, and we will get engaged. He wants to get married right away, so we have to arrange for the wedding during the time he's home. Nothing big or fancy, just simple and quick. After that, we'll leave to go wherever he's stationed. Will you help me set all of that up with the pastor? His parents said they'll help, too."

Violet looked at Henry, then said to Savannah, "This is happening so quickly dear, are you sure you don't want to take time to think about it all? Are you sure this is what you want?"

"Yes, Mama, I'm sure," replied Savannah. "When I saw Jimmy again after being away from him for twelve weeks, it was amazing. And after seeing how he changed, how he matured, my heart just melted. It was like everything I felt for him just went to a whole different level. He is perfect for me, Mama. Please help me make this happen."

Sammi Jo was listening to the conversation, uncharacteristically quiet. It was hard for her to understand how a few months ago Savannah was dating both Jimmy and Luca, and now she was so in love with Jimmy that she was willing to marry him in a rush, not even knowing where they would be moving to or what he was going to be doing. She had always thought Jimmy Simmons was a nice guy, but he had never really paid attention to her like Luca had, so she felt like she didn't really know him. Now, apparently, he was going to be her brother-in-law.

Things sure moved fast sometimes in relationships. Maybe absence really did make the heart grow fonder.

The next sixty days was a blur of wedding preparations, endless phone conversations between Savannah and Jimmy, and weekly wedding planning dinners with Jimmy's parents. They really were very nice and humble people who seemed to genuinely like Savannah. Still, Sammi Jo felt on the outside of all of it. Most of the time she just stayed out of the way, minding her own business.

Sammi Jo spent a lot of time out of the house with Bobby. Things were going well but had seemed to hit a lull. Football season was drawing to a close and all Bobby could talk about was the upcoming playoffs. The team was assured of a playoff spot, but their seeding would be low. Bobby was hoping to finish the season strong so he could attract the attention of some Division II college recruiters.

"I really need a scholarship," Bobby said, "and if I can impress the college recruiters by playing well in the playoffs, who knows? I might get a shot!"

"Don't you think you're putting too much pressure on yourself?" asked Sammi Jo. "You just need to focus on winning and executing every play. You can't go out there trying to impress people in the stands. That's a recipe for disaster. Just be yourself and focus on the team, what will happen will happen."

Bobby looked at her like she had burst his bubble. "No, I can't leave this up to chance. I have to take control of my own destiny. This is my one shot. If I don't have a deal signed by the end of my junior year it may be too late. The time is now. Why are you being so negative?"

"I'm not being negative," replied Sammi Jo. "I just know from baseball that if you try too hard, squeeze the bat too tight, you'll strike out. In baseball, they say you can't hit a five-run homerun. The same is true for football. Just go out there and play your game. You are really good. They will see that, just have faith."

"Stop with the baseball nonsense," said Bobby, "football is different. It's a real game, not a pastime. You have to be tough, and determined, and trying hard, and giving it your all really matters. Football is aggressive, baseball is passive. Football is active, baseball is reactive. I need to take control and make things happen. Just support me and encourage me or leave me alone."

Sammi Jo was really hurt by Bobby's response. She had just been trying to help him see that his focus on himself might hurt his performance and the team. His comments about baseball seemed designed to hurt her, since he knew that she loved the game. She asked herself, was there more to all of this than just the pressure of the playoffs and scholarships?

"You know what, Bobby," replied Sammi Jo, getting up from her seat at Shorty's where they had gone for dinner, "maybe it's better if I leave you alone until the playoffs are over. You obviously don't care about what I have to say, and you're going to do things your own way. I don't want you blaming me if things don't go the way you want them to go. So, let's just not see each other until it's over. After that, we can see where this relationship goes."

She gave him a kiss on the top of his head as he sat looking stunned. As she headed to the door, she said over her shoulder, "I hope you get everything you want, but I still think you are going about this the wrong way."

CHAPTER EIGHTEEN

—————◇—————

The wedding day came more quickly than Sammi Jo could have imagined. When Jimmy came home, he immediately came to the house and gave Savannah a pretty little diamond ring right there in the kitchen. The next day, they went to Raleigh to get their wedding license and got married the following Saturday.

The reception was held at the church fellowship hall, and the next day, Savannah and Jimmy were off to California. Jimmy had chosen recon as his MOS and was now going to be stationed at Camp Pendleton in San Diego, California. He had arranged for housing on base, and they needed to get out there as soon as possible to buy furniture and set the house up before Jimmy's recon training began.

And just like that, Savannah was gone.

Sammi Jo felt like she never really had the chance to tell her everything she had wanted to say before she left. With all the fast-paced wedding preparations, the engagement, the quick wedding shower, and the blur of the wedding itself, there just wasn't the time or opportunity. Even though Sammi Jo was in the wedding, she felt more like a decoration than a bridesmaid, kind of like the flowers around the church. They were important to have there, but no one really paid attention to them. After the wedding, you just throw them away, and only remember them when you look at the pictures of the day.

Sammi Jo's room was a mess. The hectic pace of the wedding and the events afterward had left the whole house in a state of disarray. She decided to start putting some of her clothes back in the closet so she could comfortably lay in her bed and read. After she had gotten most of them hung back up, she noticed an envelope stuck behind her pillow, wedged between the headboard and the mattress. It must have fallen there last night when she got into bed in the dark, exhausted from the day.

She sat on the edge of the bed and opened the envelope. It was a letter from Savannah.

Sammi Jo,

I know these past couple of months have been a whirlwind. You and I have not had as much time together as I would have liked. I am sorry for that, but remember, I'm not gone forever, just away for a while. I'm starting a new chapter of my life, which still includes you.

I believe that the last few months have brought us closer than ever before, and I wouldn't trade a minute of it for anything. I have seen such changes in you. You are quickly becoming the woman that I always knew you would be.

I know you think I'm a dunce because I had such a hard time understanding the poems of Lord Byron at first. What you don't know is that I continued reading them after the first night you helped me understand how to do it. That night truly changed my life.

I know you remember how I finally understood how Luca felt about me, and that helped me get the courage to be truthful with him.

What you don't know is that Lord Byron's writings also helped me understand my love for Jimmy. They made me realize that one way to love anything is to realize that it may be lost. I thought about that for a few days afterward and eventually realized it was true about me and Jimmy. While he was here, I had no fear he would ever be lost to me. When he left for the service, I realized that he truly could be lost to me forever, and it made me understand how much I loved him. I think it was the same for him.

I also read a few days later, "Friendship may, and often does, grow into love, but love never subsides into friendship." That quote also made me realize that my friendship with Jimmy had grown into love, and because of that, it could never return to what it once was. We had to move forward in love or not at all. That helped me make my decision. So you can see, sweet sister, that I am with Jimmy now as his wife in part because of you. You and Lord Byron helped to open my eyes. For that, I will be forever grateful.

I will end with a few more quotes from Lord Byron, "Have not all past human beings parted, and must not all the present, one day part?" This is true of us. But our parting is only temporary. We will see each other many times over the years, and each time will be a joy. As the poet says, "'Tis sweet to know there is an eye will mark our coming, and look brighter when we come." Our reunions will be more joyful now because of our parting.

Finally, Sammi Jo, remember that I love you and will be there for you no matter how far away I am. Don't be sad, you have a lot of joy ahead of you. I know you may be feeling some of the sadness I feel too, but remember what Byron said about a broken heart, "The heart will break, but broken live on."

Thank you for everything you have done for me. I will never forget.
Always, your very loving sister,
Savannah

After finishing the astonishing letter from Savannah, Sammi Jo broke down in tears. She could never have imagined that one night of bonding with her sister would have led to such life-altering changes for all of them. On one hand, she was happy to have had such a positive impact on Savannah's life. On the other hand, she was upset because it had resulted in such changes in her own. Savannah's quick departure had left an emptiness in Sammi Jo's life. Savannah had become a source of advice and understanding as she struggled to transform herself. Who would help her choose just the right clothes for each occasion? Who would help her with her makeup? Who would she sit with to talk about what a pain Bobby was sometimes?

She had no clue who would fill that void, so she got undressed, got under the covers, and cried herself to sleep thinking about the incredible power of poetry.

CHAPTER NINETEEN

───────◇───────

The next day, Sammi Jo wrote a letter to Luca. She had a few poems that she wanted him to read and evaluate, but most of all, she wanted to tell him about Savannah and Jimmy. Maybe he had some words of advice to help her deal with her sense of loss.

She was also thinking about getting his advice on the last few months with Bobby. Since she had left him sitting alone in Shorty's, things had not gone well. The team had gotten past the first game in the state playoffs but got crushed in the second game. Bobby had thrown three interceptions trying to force the ball to receivers who weren't open. He also lost his cool and was yelling at the team in the huddle near the end of the game.

The following week, Bobby was a ghost. He didn't talk to anyone at school, even Sammi Jo. Especially Sammi Jo. He was definitely avoiding her. This hurt tremendously, because Sammi Jo actually wanted the chance to comfort him and talk him through it all. Savannah had said to just leave him alone, and he would come around. That never happened, and now Savannah was gone, and Sammi Jo had no one to talk to about what to do next. She took out her stationary and began to write.

Hey Luca,

I hope you have been well since my last letter. I loved the poems you sent and read them both multiple times, and each time got more out of them. You are so amazing at creating word pictures. I am still trying to get better at that. Could you read the two poems I have included with this letter and let me know how I can make them better? The first one is called, "There's a Rainbow in my Garden" and the second one is "My House is in Wake Forest". I know they're silly and simple but hey, I'm just starting! Let me know what you think.

Also, I wanted to fill you in on Savannah and Jimmy. They got married a few days ago here in Wake Forest, and it all happened really quickly. When Savannah went with Jimmy's parents to his graduation from boot camp, he told her how much he missed her and loved her and that being apart made him realize that he didn't want to live without her. They decided to get married when he finished MCT. That took sixty days. He came home, they got engaged and then married the following Saturday. Now they're heading to San Diego. They'll be living on base at Camp Pendleton.

This has all happened so fast, and I feel surprisingly lost without her around. She has been such a source of advice and strength for me recently, and now she's gone. I have no one else to talk to about this, so I hope you don't mind if I talk to you about "stuff". You are so deep and seem to understand so much about so many things. I'm hoping you won't mind helping me out sometimes.

For example, I think I have really messed things up with Bobby. I gave him some advice which he didn't take the way I meant it. He may have really messed up his chances for a scholarship and I think he now blames me. He won't see me or talk with me, and I don't know what to do to make it better. Any advice? I hope you aren't too upset about the Savannah stuff.

Sammi Jo

Luca got Sammi Jo's letter a few days later. He was still living at his parents' house while he waited for a final decision on where he would be playing next summer. He had spent the months since the season ended with the Bulls staying in shape by working out at the gym where he had gotten a job as a fitness coach. It paid okay, but its real value to him was the access to the weight room and the other exercise equipment.

After the phone call with Savannah, he had started working out like a man possessed. He couldn't recall a time when he felt so driven to be better. Even during college, his baseball skills had come so naturally that he didn't pay enough attention to working out. But after a season in the minors, he realized how much better he needed to get. Some of his teammates were huge and it bothered him a bit. So he committed the off season to physical self-improvement. He was going to start next season, wherever he played, bigger and faster than ever before.

He made himself a protein drink in the blender and sat down on the couch in the living room to read the letter from Sammi Jo. As he read the letter, he couldn't help smiling to himself. He was happy that she appreciated his writing. Since he rarely shared anything he wrote with anyone, it was always a relief to hear that what he had written was well received, no matter who the person was that read it. But this was special because he had been the one to introduce Sammi Jo to the beauty of poetry. He certainly knew that no one else would ever describe him as "deep", and his ability to create word pictures was nowhere near the skills of the classic poets; still, it made him smile. He was glad he could impress her.

He was startled to read the news about Savannah and Jimmy. Not that it was totally a shock, what surprised him was how fast it had gone. It definitely hurt a bit to remember that Savannah had not been truthful with him from the start, but then again, he had never asked if she was dating someone else; that was his own fault. He also could not truthfully say that he had fallen in love with her, but he had definitely been smitten and was looking forward to exploring the relationship further.

As he had thought about it over the last few months, he understood that the hurt had been more about his ego, rather than the choice Savannah had made. That and the fact that he really enjoyed the Jacksons as a family. The thought that he might never see any of them again had been a big part of the hurt. Hearing again from Sammi Jo helped to mitigate that pain to some degree. It kept the connection alive, and for some reason, he felt that was important to him, but he was not sure why.

He was also very happy that Sammi Jo felt connected to him enough to reach out to him despite all that happened with Savannah and comfortable enough to ask for his advice. He had always felt that she was special. Someone who seemed so confident in her own skin yet willing to accept the need for growth and change. He felt that was unique, and he felt privileged to be asked to step in and assist her toward that end. He knew he definitely could give Sammi Jo some valuable perspective on her relationship with the high school athlete that she was dating, since he had been one himself. He would just need more facts.

When he had finished reading the letter, he unfolded the two poems Sammi Jo had included and began to read. The first one he opened was "There's a Rainbow in my Garden".

There's a rainbow in my garden
I saw it there today

While watering the plants and shrubs,
Uncovered by the spray

There's a rainbow in my garden
That only I can see
I coaxed it out of hiding
To put on a show for free

I wondered how it got there
Did it lose its way?
Was there perhaps some purpose
To its visit here today?

As I stood there spraying
Considering this sight,
Suddenly it came to me
Like a flash of pure white light

To comprehend the meaning of
Its visit was not hard
It was showing me that all I need
Is in my own backyard.

By the time Luca finished reading the poem, he was beaming. While he had been reading it, he had been transported and was easily able to visualize everything Sammi Jo had described. In his mind, he had been standing there next to her, watching her water her garden and could clearly see the rainbow that the spray from the hose revealed.

He also loved the conclusion she had drawn from the experience. On the surface, she had used her backyard as a metaphor for home and was saying that she didn't need to go searching the world for what made her happy. The important things in life can always be found at home. But he saw more in it, maybe more than Sammi Jo herself realized. He felt that it was a way of describing herself. She was both the garden and the person watering it. The more she cared for herself and took responsibility for her own growth and development, the more happiness she could expect from life. That sometimes we have to stop and notice the beauty that is always there in our lives if we just take the time to appreciate it. He was very impressed with her development. She really was becoming a talented and creative writer.

He quickly unfolded the other poem, anxious to read it after being so encouraged by the first one. He read the title, "My House is in Wake Forest".

My house is in Wake Forest
A lovely place to see
With rolling hills and horse farms
Green grass and ancient trees

My house is in Wake Forest
Friends and family live there too
We share our hopes, we share our dreams
We share a bond that's true

My house is in Wake Forest
And no matter where I roam
With all the love that's living there
It will always be my home.

Once again, he was grinning. Well done, Sammi Jo, he thought to himself. Once again, you have transported me right there to your hometown with very few words.

When he thought about the first poem and its message,

along with the meaning of the second one, he got the sense that Sammi Jo was on the verge of change. That she was starting to be reflective and appreciative of all she had experienced growing up in her little town with such a great family. To him, that signaled that she was starting to think about the future and to recognize that things might not always be as simple as they had been. That she was going to have to go out into a world that might not be as cozy and comforting as the one she might someday have to leave behind.

In his mind, he saw the image of a caterpillar starting to create the cocoon into which it would have to retreat to begin the transformation into the butterfly it must one day become. In doing so, the butterfly closes itself off to all it has known before, lives in darkness and silence for a long time before the transformation is complete. During that dark time, what the caterpillar experiences must feel like a form of death in which its thoughts are all about the wonderful and comforting things it experienced before entering the cocoon and has now lost. It cannot know, it cannot even imagine, all of the wonderful and undreamed-of experiences that await it when the metamorphosis is complete.

As he put the letter and the poems aside, thinking about all he had read, he was sure that this was what Sammi Jo was feeling and had unknowingly expressed through her writings. He knew that he wanted to be there when she completed her metamorphosis. It would be a sight to see!

He also suddenly recognized that he, too, was going through changes.

As he thought about his baseball career, he could see that he was still a caterpillar in some ways. Sure, maybe he was an older, more mature caterpillar, but he was still crawling on the ground. If he was ever going to get to the major leagues, he was going to have to change. Get bigger, stronger, and grow some wings. He began to see the minors as a sort of cocoon, as his opportunity to change and grow. He knew that caterpillars, after entering the cocoon and going through all the internal changes that they experience while in there, eventually have to struggle mightily to escape from the restrictive confines they have created for themselves. It is that struggle, that battle to break free, that is the final test. No one can do it for the butterfly; it has to do it for itself, or it will never fly.

He took out some stationary and began to write his reply to Sammi Jo.

CHAPTER TWENTY

Summer 1981

Sammi Jo was a fixture at almost every Durham Bulls home game the next summer. She hated to admit it to Luca, but she was thrilled when he had written back to her and told her that the Savannah Braves had not picked up his contract and that he would be back with the Durham Bulls for the 1981 season. She also had found it interesting that Luca hadn't seemed as distraught as she'd assumed he would be about that. When they had spoken about it, he made a bunch of references to caterpillars and cocoons and butterflies which she did not understand at all.

She was also speechless, the first time she saw him that summer, at the physical changes in him. He had gotten so much stronger and muscular. He almost crushed her when he gave her a great, big, "hello" bear hug. Luca was not the tallest guy, the program listed him at five feet eleven inches, but to Sammi Jo he looked like he was at least two inches taller. She had to admit, she kind of liked it. He looked incredible.

He told her that he had already allocated all of his free passes to her and her family, and they could come to the ballpark anytime they wanted, free of charge. The seats were right behind the dugout along the first base line, and

Sammi Jo took advantage of Luca's generosity as often as possible, both with and without her parents.

Early on, she brought Bobby to a few of the games. Things had gotten straightened out between them a few weeks after Bobby's disastrous playoff performance. Luca's advice had really helped Sammi Jo work through all of that. He had told her to stay away from him because he was actually going through a grieving process. From experience, he knew that young athletes take significant losses very hard, especially when they believe that their future was dependent upon winning. She recognized the truth in this and followed Luca's advice.

Over time, Bobby started to come around. At first, he would stop by her locker occasionally just to say hello. Then he started calling at night just to talk. Eventually, they were dating again, and things were comfortable, but never exactly the same.

Bobby had not gotten any scholarship offers by the end of junior year, but he was still hopeful that if he had a great senior year, he might attract some attention from a smaller division two or maybe a quality division three school. Sammi Jo encouraged this hope, and that seemed to help. Unfortunately, she had still not been able to nurture any love of baseball in him. After the first few games, she began to grow tired of his constant criticism of the game, so she stopped asking him to come with her. Besides, she really enjoyed going by herself. She could concentrate on the game, analyze Luca's performance, and really get to know some of the other players on the team.

But most of all, she *really* loved going out to dinner with Luca after the games. Luca had gotten permission from her daddy and mama after the first home game when he gave her a ride home. They had all been sitting around talking about the game, and Luca really enjoyed Sammi Jo's analysis and insight. He said that he would like to talk with her after every game and came up with the idea of after-game dinner sessions. Knowing Luca and trusting him so much, her dad agreed to let her try it a couple of times and see how it went.

One of the best things that came out of that situation was that her daddy had surprised her with a car of her own as an early seventeenth birthday present, so she could get to and from the ballpark and drive herself to work.

Sammi Jo had gotten a job for the summer at a small daycare center. She loved working with the children and the hours were great. She was done by three p.m. and didn't have to work on weekends, so she could get to the night games and every weekend game.

None of that seemed to bother Bobby all that much, since he spent most of his time working out. She had suggested to Bobby that he talk with Luca about his recommendations for working out, since it had made such a change in him, but Bobby refused. He said there was nothing that a baseball player could teach him about working out, so Sammi Jo dropped it. They still dated during the week but only on nights when there wasn't a Bulls home game. Sammi Jo was okay with that.

Sammi Jo had become a real fixture at the ballpark, and many of the Bulls players started thinking of her as their good luck charm, because they were having a great season. They had only lost two home games through the first half. Many of them would pass her their bats or helmets to touch before getting into the on-deck circle, and she loved it. It made her feel like a part of the team. She got to know every player by name, and they all knew her and made her feel very special.

Luca was also having a breakout season. He was starting to hit for power now in addition to having a great batting average. They moved him to the number three spot in the lineup, and he was killing it. Sammi Jo was a little flustered, because she was not spotting any flaws in his swing and had nothing to offer Luca in the way of advice. Still, he always asked for her observations when they went to dinner after the games.

One night while they were having dinner after a game where Luca went four-for-four with three RBIs and a home run, he once again asked her if she saw anything wrong with his swing.

"Are you kidding me?" Sammi Jo responded. "You just had a career game. What could possibly be wrong with your swing?"

Luca smiled. "Hey, you never know. I've learned that you can't rest on your laurels. There's always a flaw somewhere, there's always something to improve. I can't see it myself, so I have to have someone who really knows me point it out. That's you, Sammi Jo. I trust you to tell me when I'm not at my best."

"See," said Sammi Jo, "that's the difference between you and Bobby. He doesn't trust that I can make a valid observation or give him any good advice. He's convinced that he always knows what's best. He even has a hard time taking advice from the coaches. If he had listened to me, he might have a scholarship in his pocket today. Why is that Luca? Why can't he trust me to help him?"

"Some young guys are like that," said Luca. "I'm sure I was like that too when I was younger, to some extent. I was lucky, though; my dad was a great teacher. I learned early on to trust him completely. It made me open to listening to others. He always told me that if someone was willing to take the time to offer a suggestion to help me improve, that I should at least give it a try. I didn't always have to use the advice they gave me, but I needed to have enough respect to at least consider it. That's been a huge help in my career. It even applies to my writing. I actually see the same quality in you, Sammi Jo, you are very open to advice."

"Why do you say that?" asked Sammi Jo.

"Because," replied Luca, "you ask for my advice on your writing, which is a very personal thing. If you are willing to take criticism and advice on something so personal, then it means that you are open to it in other areas of your life. Also, Savannah had filled me in on your commitment to personal growth and how you took to heart everything she told you to do. I can see how much you have changed since last summer. You've really matured into a sweet young lady in a truly short time. That's no small accomplishment. Especially because you haven't lost any of the real Sammi Jo while doing it."

Sammi Jo was glad that the lighting in the restaurant was low, because she felt herself blushing. This startled her, because she had never blushed before when talking with Luca. She had always thought of him as a sort of older brother figure, and nothing he had ever said had caused her to blush. Why now, she wondered as she took a drink of water to calm herself.

"Luca, do you mind if I go to the ladies' room for a minute?" she asked as she stood from her chair.

"Of course not," said Luca, a bit confused. "Did I say something to upset you?"

"No, not at all," replied Sammi Jo. "If the waiter comes, just order me a hamburger well done and I'll be back in a minute."

As Sammi Jo walked away, Luca couldn't help but feel

that he embarrassed her somehow. He felt that he knew her well enough to figure that out, but why it happened was a mystery. He also couldn't help but notice that other guys in the restaurant were watching Sammi Jo as she passed by on her way to the ladies' room. That bothered him. What were they looking at? She was a sweet young girl, and they needed to keep their eyes to themselves.

The waiter came while Sammi Jo was gone and Luca ordered two hamburgers, well done, with a beer for himself and a sweet tea for Sammi Jo. Before the waiter left, he said to Luca, "Nice game today. I was at the ballpark earlier and was very impressed. You're really having a great season. Your date must be proud."

"Thanks," said Luca, "but she's not my date. She's just a friend who gives me batting advice."

The waiter raised an eyebrow. "Really? Well, then maybe you wouldn't mind if I ask her out and let her help me with my swing? She's really hot," he said with a wink.

Luca stood from his chair and decked the guy.

Then he took some money from his wallet and threw it at the guy. "Next time, just take the order and keep your mouth shut."

Luca looked up and saw Sammi Jo, who had paused on the edge of the room on her way back to their table, a bewildered look on her face as she took in the scene. He approached her.

"Come on, Sammi Jo," he said as he took her by the arm. "Looks like we are going to Char Grill. The atmosphere there is much better." Some of the patrons of the restaurant started to applaud as he led her out.

When they were outside, Sammi Jo asked, "What happened in there? What was that all about?"

"Nothing," replied Luca, "he just needed to learn some manners, and he wasn't very coachable."

CHAPTER TWENTY-ONE

Sammi Jo continued to attend as many home games as possible, always enjoying the after-game dinners with Luca, relieved that there had been no further "coaching" incidents. Luca never did explain fully to Sammi Jo why it had happened, so she just assumed it was a "guy thing" and forgot about it. What she didn't forget about was blushing during their conversation, which still confused her.

Luca had become increasingly chivalrous when they ate together, opening doors, holding her chair for her, helping her with her sweater, things like that. She had told him that none of it was necessary, but he insisted, telling her that it was behavior that she should expect from any guy that was worthy of her. He was modeling what he felt she should demand and expect. Of course, they always talked about baseball and every dinner started off with an inning by inning review of the game. Sammi Jo loved it because as a fan, she was able to give him her perception of the game from the outside in. Then she got to hear Luca's explanation of the same game from the inside out. She was really learning and that excited her.

But over time, the dinners became increasingly about poetry and writing. Sammi Jo liked the fact that she could get instant feedback on her poems and actually discuss them in person with Luca shortly after she had written them.

Even more than that, she enjoyed reading what he wrote. Some of what he shared with her were poems that were in various stages of composition. Some were just ideas, others were outlines, and others were complete. It gave her such insight into the creative process and how Luca's mind worked. That was great, but what was even more fun was feeling the excitement and passion emanating from him during their discussions.

Often when they discussed baseball and specific games, he was passionate and intense, but it was a serious passion that was about learning and analysis. But when they discussed poetry, his passion came across as enjoyment and recreation. He was animated, enthusiastic, and spirited, and that energized Sammi Jo. She resonated with his zeal for writing, and his passion fed hers. They often lost track of time during these conversations, but neither seemed to mind, or have anything else they would prefer to do, or any place they would rather be.

Luca insisted that she read her creations to him out loud. He said it really mattered because only she could impart the proper emphasis and inflections she intended. That was fine with Sammi Jo most of the time, but recently, as her writings had started to evolve to be more about her feelings, she started to experience a little reluctance. Tonight was one of those times.

"Seriously, Sammi Jo, read it to me," encouraged Luca. "I've told you before how important it is for me to hear it from you. I want to feel your emotions as you read. I need to understand what you were feeling as you wrote it. I can make a better evaluation that way."

"But this one is different," Sammi Jo replied. "It's not about family, or school or my town or friends, it's

113

different."

"Different how?" asked Luca.

"It's about love… sort of," Sammi Jo tried to explain. "I mean, it's what I think love will be like someday. It's kind of a wish or a hope or a dream of love. It's a little embarrassing to share it with you."

"Why would it be embarrassing to share what you've written or what you feel with me?" asked Luca. "Have I ever made you feel bad about anything you have ever shared with me?"

"No," replied Sammi Jo, "but I've always written about stuff that I have firsthand knowledge of. This is different. I don't think I've ever really experienced romantic love, and I know that you have. You may think it's juvenile or silly and laugh at me."

"I would never do that, Sammi Jo," replied Luca, reaching across the table and resting his hand on hers. "You and I have trust between us. That means that we always tell each other the truth. If you hadn't been straight with me the first time you told me about dropping my shoulder, we wouldn't be here today. I promise that whatever you share with me, I will give you my truthful assessment. Do you have enough faith in me to believe that?"

"I do," Sammi Jo responded hesitantly. "You're right, I'm just being silly. Just let me get through it before you say anything, or I might not want to finish it, okay? And don't look at me while I'm reading it."

"Okay," agreed Luca. "I always like to know the ground rules before the game begins."

Sammi Jo took out the poem and took a deep breath. As she read it over before beginning, she felt her face flushing. She was really glad she had told Luca not to look at her while she read. With her heart beating wildly, she began.

"Fairy Tales Come True," she started, reading the title.

I've chased a lot of rainbows
And even caught a few
But every pot of gold I've found
I'd give away for you

I've rubbed a lot of magic lamps
Seen genies by the score
But for every wish they've granted me
You've granted even more

Did you know that you're my Camelot?
My Lancelot so fair
And every day when I awake
There's magic in the air

I've read about Atlantis
Heard the mermaid's laughter
But you'll always be my fairytale
My happily ever after.

Sammi Jo finished reading and kept looking down at the paper. She was embarrassed to even look at Luca, afraid he might be laughing, or scowling or even wincing in pain. She waited for him to say something, but nothing came. Had he left? Had it been so bad that he left the table to go to the bathroom and throw up? She summoned all of her courage and looked up from the paper. Luca was sitting still, staring at his hands folded in front of him.

"Luca," Sammi Jo said, "Are you all right? Was it that bad?"

Luca looked up. She saw that his eyes were rimmed in

red and that he was also flushed a bit. He said, "Sammi Jo, that was beautiful. It was simple, pure, real, and so hopeful. Really, I think Lord Byron would be jealous."

Sammi Jo finally exhaled. "Do you really think so? Seriously?"

"Seriously," replied Luca. "You made me connect with what you were saying. You made me think about the first blush of love and how I have felt that in the past. About the feelings a new love stirs in the heart and mind, and the dreams that come with it, and the hopes for the future. You captured all of that so perfectly. But for me as the listener, I also felt the crushing pain of losing that 'Camelot', seeing those dreams crumble before my eyes. That, Sammi Jo, is what poetry is about, inspiring those personal feelings in your audience, and you did that to perfection. Do *not* change a word, do you understand?"

"I won't," replied Sammi Jo. "But do you think I'll find that kind of love someday?"

"I'm sure you will, Sammi Jo," replied Luca. "You have already put it down on paper, and when we put our feelings, even wishes, into words, they seem to find a way to come true. But, even if it comes and doesn't look exactly like this at the beginning, you can work towards it. You can love it into being. You can create your own happily ever after. That is something I believe with all my heart."

"I hope you're right, Luca," sighed Sammi Jo. "I will keep on dreaming."

"I hope it for both of us, slugger," replied Luca. "Let's keep encouraging each other's dreams and keep on swinging. Then both of us can have our own fairytales come true. Deal?" he asked as he reached his hand across the table.

Sammi Jo took his hand in hers, shook it, and said, "Deal."

CHAPTER TWENTY-TWO

⬥

The Bulls' 1981 season had ended in disappointment. Even though they were at the top of the league all season long, pitching had once again failed them in the playoffs. They lost in the first round to a much less talented Winston-Salem team. Sammi Jo was at every home playoff game and had rubbed so many helmets and bats that her hands were raw and stained with pine tar. The team had hit well but just could not manufacture enough runs to make up for the subpar pitching.

Luca had a great playoff performance, hitting well, and was flawless in the field. He ended the season in the top five in the league in batting average and in the top twenty in home runs and RBIs. This softened the blow of the early exit from the playoffs, and Luca was optimistic about the prospect of moving up to the AA Savannah Braves the following season. Sammi Jo was happy for him but dreaded the thought of not having him around.

Before he left to head north for the off season, Luca came by the house to say goodbye to Henry, Violet, and Casey, and pick up Sammi Jo for their last dinner together.

"Luca!" exclaimed Henry as he hustled him into the kitchen. "So good to see you, son. What a great season you had. So sorry about the playoffs, but hey, at least you did your part. No one could put any of the blame on you. Would you like a last glass of Violet's sweet tea before you head home?"

"Absolutely," replied Luca. "I definitely miss it during the off season."

Henry went to the refrigerator and took out the always full pitcher of sweet tea. As he was pouring a glass for Luca and then himself, he asked, "So, have you heard anything from the AA team in Savannah? They must be chomping at the bit to bring you up there next season."

Accepting the glass from Henry and taking a quick sip he replied, "Yes, actually, this afternoon. They've picked up my contract for next season. I have to report a little earlier than usual to have a physical done and go through some sort of orientation, so the off season will be a little shorter for me this year. But I'm really excited. I can't believe my dream is starting to come true."

"Well, you've earned it," said Henry, clinking glasses with Luca. "Congratulations. We'll miss you. I assume you haven't told Sammi Jo yet, since you just found out this afternoon. She's sure going to take it hard. Have you thought about how you're going to tell her?"

"Not really, Henry," Luca replied, putting his glass down on the coffee table. "Maybe you have some advice for me?"

Henry chuckled. "I don't envy you, son, you've become such a fixture in her life. She looks forward to every game and really enjoys the dinners with you. You not being here will leave a big hole in her summer next year. What I suggest is that you assure her that you'll still stay in touch and give her a vision of something else to fill the hole. Get her excited about something different, something new, a way to channel her energy. She really respects your advice, and with Savannah gone, she needs that. Does that help?"

"Yes, it does, Henry," replied Luca, "The problem is figuring out what that something else is."

Sammi Jo entered the living room from her bedroom where she had been dressing. Seeing Luca and her daddy sitting there talking gave her a sick feeling in her stomach, which she quickly ignored.

"Luca!" she said as she went to him and gave him a big hug. "You did so well in that last game! I just know if you had only gotten that last at bat, you would've won the game for the team."

"Really?" said Luca, "Didn't you learn anything from 'Casey at the Bat'? Sometimes the last guy up still can't make it happen. I am kind of glad it wasn't me that made the last out, or you would be writing about 'Luca at the Bat'! Not sure I could deal with that." Sammi Jo laughed at the thought.

"My, how dressed up you are," remarked Luca noticing the very pretty outfit she was wearing. "Have you decided to take me somewhere fancy tonight?"

"Dinner is on me tonight, Luca," interjected Henry. "A sort of thank you for all the tickets you gave us this year and congratulations for such a great season. Sammi Jo is going to take you to Vinnie's, the best steak house in Raleigh. I know you'll love it. Have fun."

Sammi Jo was so excited. She had never been to Vinnie's before but had heard so much about it. "Thank you, Daddy," said Sammi Jo, hugging him, "this is going to be so much fun! Luca, are you ready to go?"

"Not yet," said Luca, "I need to say goodbye to your mom. Where is she?"

"She was over at her mama's house," Henry answered.

"She will be here shortly. More sweet tea, Luca?" As Henry was walking into the kitchen, Violet and her mama came through the door.

"Luca!" Violet greeted him with a smile. "I was so worried we would miss you. It takes Granny a little longer these days to walk up the driveway. I hope we haven't kept you."

"No, ma'am," replied Luca, giving her a big bear hug and a kiss on the cheek. "I wouldn't leave without seeing you. You've been my substitute mother while I've been here."

"I would like you to finally meet Sammi Jo and Savannah's granny," said Violet motioning to her mama, "Missus Annie Baker."

Luca turned to greet Granny, but before he could say anything, she said, "So, I hear you are the kind of boy who likes to date sisters."

Clearly taken aback a bit, Luca looked at Violet, who was starting to smile, "Granny can be a little direct. She may bark, but she doesn't bite," she said. "Just go with it."

Luca responded, "No ma'am, I mean, I did date Savannah for a while, but I am not dating Sammi Jo, we're just friends."

"That's not what it looks like to me," replied Granny. "In my day, if you went to dinner every week with the same person, *alone*, that was dating. Have you kissed her?"

Luca was starting to sweat, and he stammered, "Of course not, we're friends and she's only seventeen!"

Granny looked him dead in the eye and said, "So what? I was the same age as Sammi Jo when Luther and I got married, and he was a little older than you. I had Violet by the time I was eighteen. I don't understand why young people these days wait till they're all grown to get married, where's the fun in that?"

Sammi Jo was now blushing once again and starting to sweat. Violet was covering her mouth trying not to laugh and Henry had left the room to avoid the fallout. Luca looked stricken, not knowing how to respond.

Violet finally stepped in and got Luca off the hook. "Mama, the kids need to get going. They have dinner reservations, and we're making them late."

"Okay," Granny replied, "but I will never understand how a handsome young man like this can have dinner every week with a beautiful young girl like Sammi Jo and not want to marry her and make beautiful babies as quickly as possible." Then she shook her head and retreated to the kitchen.

Violet took a completely embarrassed Luca by the elbow and started to lead him out the door. Sammi Jo followed. She gave her granny a hug as she passed her and whispered in her ear, "It's not like that, Granny, we're just good friends."

"Hogwash!" Granny replied. "My eyes are still good, and I can see that there's more here than either of you want to admit. One of you better open your eyes, or you will regret it, mark my words."

Sammi Jo gave her a kiss on the cheek and followed her mama and Luca out to the car. Violet and Luca were standing by the car laughing hysterically. When Sammi Jo got there, she asked, "What's so funny?"

Her mama replied through tears of laughter, "I knew she was in an ornery mood today, but I had no idea she was going to say all of that. I am so sorry; I know that must have been embarrassing."

Luca, still trying to regain his composure, said, "Well, at least I have a great story to tell when I get home. She is really something. Does she challenge all of the guys that date your daughters that way?"

121

"I thought you said we weren't dating?" said Sammi Jo, looking confused and a little hurt. Luca stopped laughing. "I was referring to Savannah," he stammered, "I didn't mean... that I was dating both of you... I mean..."

Sammi Jo started to laugh, "See, Mama, you're right, I do have a lot of Granny in me!"

Realizing that Sammi Jo was just having fun with him, Luca started laughing again, and so did Violet.

None of them saw Granny, looking out the window at the three of them laughing by the car, or heard as she said to Henry, who had just reentered the kitchen when the coast was clear, "Yep, those young'uns are dating for sure, they just don't know it. Yes, indeed."

When they got to Vinnie's, Luca was impressed by the warm, elegant atmosphere, and the attentive and polite waiters. "Looks like I won't have to be 'coaching' anyone tonight," Luca said as he held Sammi Jo's chair for her as she sat.

"I hope not!" said Sammi Jo. "One time was enough for my taste, although you were pretty impressive. You knocked him down with one punch!"

"He only needed a short lesson," Luca responded, smiling.

The waiter came and took their drink orders and gave them their menus.

When he left, Luca said, "I got some good news today."

"Really?" replied Sammi Jo. "Did you win league MVP or something?"

"Better than that," said Luca. "I got the call from the Savannah Braves. They want me there next season and have picked up my contract."

Sammi Jo lost her breath for a moment, feeling as if she had been suddenly plunged beneath the water of an icy river, but recovered quickly. "How wonderful for you!" she said, meaning it but suddenly feeling sick inside. "Are you excited or nervous? I would be so nervous!"

Luca, examining her face for any signs of emotion, answered, "I'm not nervous, Sammi Jo, because I'm ready for this next step. But I am a bit sad because I won't have you there to coach me every day. Will you be okay?"

"Sure," replied Sammi Jo, looking down at the napkin on her lap. "I'll still go to the Bulls games, but I will just need to find another player to coach. Maybe even go to some after-game dinners with him. After all, they all saw how I turned you into an AA player so fast. I'm sure I'll have them lined up when they find out you are gone." As soon as she said that, she regretted it and felt like crying. She knew that she had said it in part to hurt him, even though she didn't mean a word of it.

Luca looked at her, smiling softly. "I'm sure you're right, any of those goons would be lucky to have you as their coach. Just stay away from that new guy Brett Butler, I don't like him," he said with a wink. "He's too good."

"He's an outfielder," said Sammi Jo. "I like infielders better."

The waiter returned, told them the specials, and took their order. Sammi Jo, having suddenly lost her appetite, ordered the smallest steak they had.

When the waiter left, Luca said, "You should have ordered the biggest steak and brought some home for Casey. He would love a Vinnie's steak!" When Sammi Jo didn't laugh, Luca knew it was time to dig deeper.

"Look, Sammi Jo, all kidding aside, I'm really going to miss you, and I think you are going to miss me, too. We can joke all we want, but we both know this is going to hurt. You and your family are the only thing that has gotten me through these first two years down here, becoming a second family to me. Before I met you all, I was pretty down on the whole experience, even thinking of quitting. If I had anything other than a literature degree, I might have done it, but my only marketable skill is baseball. You guys gave me hope. You brought the fun back to the game for me, and *you* fixed my swing! I will never forget that."

"Will you call me and write?" asked Sammi Jo, now fighting back tears.

"Of course," replied Luca. "At least once a week. I hear the travel is better, more comfortable in AA so I should get plenty of rest to be able to analyze your writing without falling asleep."

He softened his teasing with a wink. "But seriously, Sammi Jo," he continued, "you'll be starting senior year soon, and you need to start thinking about yourself, your future. Next summer, you will have graduated high school, and you have to decide now what you're going to do. Will you go to college? Will you work? There are a lot of things that you have to figure out, and the last thing you need is to be worried about me, or anyone else for that matter. It might be better without me here."

When Sammi Jo didn't respond, he continued. "What do you want to do with the rest of your life? What, besides baseball and poetry, really gets you excited?"

Sammi Jo stopped playing with her napkin and replied, "I like working with kids. I have really enjoyed working this summer at the daycare center. Maybe I can do that?"

"Sure," said Luca, "there are lots of ways to make that happen. For example, you could be a teacher. That's a wonderful career, and you would be great at it. You could teach literature!"

Sammi Jo laughed at that. "Not sure I could get third graders interested in Lord Byron," she said jokingly.

"Then start with 'Casey at the Bat'!" said Luca. "Kids love that one."

"I know. This *kid* really liked it, too," Sammi Jo replied, giving him another little dig. "Do you think I could be a coach? Do colleges have degrees for that?"

"Absolutely," replied Luca. "That would be a great option. In fact, North Carolina State has a great physical education program, and I know the baseball coach there. He helps out with the Bulls sometimes. I could get you an appointment to talk with him about it. Would you like that?"

Sammi Jo brightened a bit at the suggestion. "Sure, that would be great. Maybe he'll even let me help out with the baseball team if I go there. I'm sure some of his players could benefit from my coaching."

Once again, she regretted saying that as soon as it was out of her mouth. She knew Luca didn't have any other choice; still, it seemed to her like he was trying to distract her from the obvious, that he was leaving her and moving on.

The waiter returned with their food and conversation halted. When the waiter retreated, Sammi Jo found the courage to continue. "Luca, I'm sorry. I keep saying that I can find another player to coach. I don't mean it. I'm just sad and a little angry. This really hurts. I knew it was coming, but now that it's here, it hurts more than I thought it would. I will take your advice, I will move on to other things and focus on my future, but that doesn't mean that I'm going to forget you or feel any different about you. I hope you feel the same."

Luca reached across the table and took her hand. "Of course, Sammi Jo. How could I ever forget you? You're family, and I don't forget family, ever."

Sammi Jo smiled. "Good. Now, can we talk about baseball, please?"

The talk about baseball salvaged the evening, but as he

backed out of the Jacksons' driveway, Luca couldn't help but feel that things between them were going to change. Distance was a very difficult hurdle to overcome in any kind of relationship. Even though he was committed to staying in touch with Sammi Jo and her family, he knew it was going to be tough.

When he got to his apartment in Durham and parked the car, he noticed a folded piece of paper on the passenger seat. He picked it up and unfolded it. It was a poem that Sammi Jo had written that she either forgot or decided not to read to him.

It was titled "The Cold is Coming". He began to read.

The cold is coming, I cannot fight it off
The cold is coming, I can feel the winter's frost
The cold is coming and from it I can't run
The cold is coming, black clouds obscure the sun

I turn my collar to its bitter bite
And still there is no ceasing
I steel my heart against its sting
But still it keeps increasing

I long for warmth, I long for green
I long for springtime's blessings
I long to feel its warm caress
And heat upon me pressing

I pray the memories keep me strong,
Keep my heart from freezing
I pray that just the smallest glimpse
Will chase away this season.

Again I turn into the cold

And face the cruelest thought
I know the truth, the cold is coming
And I cannot fight it off.

At the bottom was a note from Sammi Jo.

Bye Luca, stay warm.
Love always,
Sammi Jo

He sat there for a long time in the passenger seat holding the poem and thinking about what Sammi Jo had written. Finally, he folded the poem, put it in his jacket pocket, and as he hustled inside to get his luggage and load the car for the trip north in the morning, he noticed for the first time how chilly the night suddenly felt.

CHAPTER TWENTY-THREE

Summer 1982

As he sat in his normal spot at the end of the Savannah Braves bench, Luca was a little frustrated, to say the least. He had yet to start a game even though the starting shortstop was hitting well below .250. He understood that the guy had been here for two years, had gotten a huge signing bonus, and had the backing of the major league team, but half of the season was over, and they should have made a change by now.

Luca had gotten some playing time, but it was sporadic, and not playing every day was something he wasn't used to. He knew he wasn't in his rhythm and needed more playing time to get there. It was a no-win situation, because when they did put him in, he was not at his best, and unless he was at his best, he was not going to take the starting job away from the current shortstop. The whole situation was taking a toll on him emotionally.

As he sat there on the bench, occupying his mind with trying to steal signals from the other bench, his mind wandered. He thought about the girl he had met two days ago.

He had been out by himself having dinner after one of the home games, and was sitting alone writing notes about the last week so he could remember the details and use it in his writing. She came up to him and asked him why he was alone and what he was doing. He explained that he was a baseball player and was just writing in his journal. Indicating that she was alone, too, she invited herself to join him for dinner and introduced herself as Cynthia.

During the conversation, she explained that she had recently relocated for her job and didn't know anyone in Savannah. The evening went well, and they found they had a few things in common, but baseball was not one of those things. She was engaging, animated, well educated, and very pretty, but Luca found her a little self-centered and forward. They exchanged phone numbers and parted company after dinner.

As he sat there thinking about her, he heard his name called. "Milano, you're pinch hitting for Ingle this inning, get ready."

Luca jumped up from his seat and all but ran to the bat rack. He grabbed his bat and his helmet and started up the steps of the dugout to the on-deck circle.

"Wake up, rookie," said the player already occupying the on-deck circle, "Ingle is batting third." Realizing his mistake, Luca returned to the dugout to the ribbing of his teammates.

I have to calm down, he told himself, and took a few breaths. I can't be thinking that any time I get out there I have to impress the coach or win the position with one at bat. That's basic. Just make contact and do the job. They'll see my ability over time. Don't press. Stay calm.

He continued to calm himself as he watched the first batter take a walk. He focused his concentration on the pitcher, watching his motion and timing his delivery.

That seemed to help a lot. He felt his mind getting back into that state it always got to when he was about to bat.

The crowd noise evaporated, and his mind started to slow down.

The guy was missing high and was having trouble throwing the curve for strikes. That meant he was going to have to slow the velocity of his fastball to get it down in the zone and couldn't depend on the curve for a late count strikeout. The second batter also walked on six pitches.

As Luca was taking his on-deck swings, he watched the opposing pitching coach walk to the mound to talk with the pitcher. Luca thought, please don't take him out, just leave him in there until I get a shot at him. I've got this guy's number. The pitching coach finished his discussion and returned to the bench, leaving the pitcher in.

Luca smiled to himself as he strode to the plate, reviewing the situation in his head. The Braves were behind four to two in the bottom of the ninth, so he knew the team had two options. One was to bunt and move the runners over into scoring position. That was the smart thing to do, but it was not his call. The coach would make that call.

The other option was to take a conservative approach and just swing for a single. That would probably score the guy at second base and move the other runner to third with nobody out. The last thing he wanted to do was pop up. Even a long fly ball might move the runner from second to third.

Before entering the batter's box, he checked the third base coach for signals. He got the take sign. As he dug in, he lifted his back elbow to remind him to keep his back shoulder level. He took the first pitch for a ball. Stepping out, he checked again for signals, receiving the take sign. The second pitch was a strike. Again, he checked and got the take signal. This confused Luca, because he fully expected the bunt sign. The opposing third baseman also assumed he would be bunting and was creeping closer. Luca took the pitch for a strike. The count was now one ball, two strikes, and he was out of options. If the pitch was close, he had to make contact. He choked up on the bat and dug in for the next pitch. It was high and tight. Two balls, two strikes. Again, he dug in, and the next pitch was high and outside. Three balls, two strikes.

Luca smiled again because he knew the pitcher didn't want to walk him and load the bases with no outs. He had just thrown Luca two blazing fast balls high and out of the zone. He was going to have to take a little off it and groove it, if he wanted to stay in the game.

As Luca dug in, he repeated to himself, calm down, just make contact and hit it up the middle. When the pitch came, it was just what Luca was anticipating, an eighty-five mile-an-hour fastball on the outer half of the plate. Luca calmly stepped into it and stroked it to right center. As he ran to first, expecting the ball to drop gently into the gap, he saw it sail over the right centerfield fence.

As Luca rounded third, he saw the team gathering around home plate. He stepped on home plate and into a gauntlet of back slaps, high fives, and helmet taps. A walk off home run, he thought as he made his way to the dugout. That is a first for me. I can't wait to tell Sammi Jo.

After the game, a few of his teammates took him out for drinks. Luca was not much of a drinker, but he didn't mind celebrating, especially since he felt so good, and it was the first time he felt that he had really contributed this season.

They ended up the evening at Kevin Barry's Irish Pub. It was a lively place along the waterfront with a live band and an incredible selection of draft Irish beer. The rounds flowed freely and quickly, and his teammates wouldn't let Luca pay for any of them. By the third round, Luca was starting to feel the effects. That's when he felt a warm breath in his ear and hair brushing his neck.

"So, what does a girl have to do to get a drink and a dance around here?" a female voice whispered in his ear. He turned around to see the smiling face of Cynthia not more than three inches from his own.

He returned her smile. "Tell me what a sacrifice fly is, and it's a done deal."

The player standing next to Luca, overhearing the comment, leaned into the conversation and said, "You don't need to answer any questions for me, sweetie, all you have to do is ask."

Seeing Cynthia tense a bit and wanting to get her away from his tipsy teammates, Luca said to Cynthia, "I'll give you half credit for effort, how about finishing the quiz on the dance floor?"

Luca spent the rest of the night there at the pub dancing with Cynthia and celebrating with his teammates, and never once remembered that he had wanted to call Sammi Jo to share his good news.

CHAPTER TWENTY-FOUR

Luca woke up the next day with a pounding headache and a massive hangover. This is why I gave up drinking, he thought to himself as he downed three aspirins and made some extra strong coffee. As he got into a steaming shower, he tried to remember how he had gotten home. None of my teammates were in any better condition to drive than me, so I must have taken a cab, he thought. Still, he couldn't remember clearly. He did recall spending the night dancing with Cynthia, but even that was a blur.

He got out of the shower, dried off, and as he was getting dressed, heard a knock on the door. He pulled on his jeans, not taking time to put on a t-shirt and answered the door. It was Cynthia, arms loaded with breakfast goodies and a bag of groceries.

"So, you are alive," she quipped as she pushed past Luca and headed toward the kitchen. "When I last saw you, you were dead to the world. Glad to see you upright and breathing. I hope you like quiche, the local bakery makes the best I've had in years."

"When did you last see me?" asked Luca, very confused.

"Last night, silly," replied Cynthia. "Don't you remember?"

"Actually, no," Luca said, scratching his head. "I don't remember much, remind me."

"You don't remember me driving you home?" she asked.

"No, I don't," replied Luca, "but thanks. I'm sure I would have been a menace on the road."

"You wouldn't have been a menace because you wouldn't have been able to get the keys into the ignition. I had to undress you to get you into bed! I doubt you could have driven, for goodness' sake!"

Luca was speechless. He tried to remember any of it and could not. "You undressed me? Seriously? Now that is embarrassing."

"Believe me, you have nothing to be embarrassed about in my estimation," she said with a wink. "In fact, I kind of enjoyed it. But my, you have an awful lot of scrapes and bruises on your legs. How did you get all of those?"

"Just a part of the game," Luca replied, pouring himself some coffee and taking a seat at the kitchen table. "Sliding, foul balls, splinters from riding the bench, all a part of the hazards of minor league baseball. What happened after you undressed me?"

"Now don't tell me you don't remember that!" complained Cynthia. "You're really going to hurt a girl's feelings."

Luca started to sweat and stammer. "I'm sorry, I don't mean to hurt your feelings, but I don't remember."

Cynthia finished setting out two plates of food and pouring more coffee for both of them and said, "Well just sit there, have something to eat, and I will fill you in."

As they ate, Cynthia said, "It's really juicy, I will remember it forever. So romantic and memorable. Do you want to hear about it?"

"Yes!" Luca exclaimed. "Come on, don't drag it out,

just tell me already, please. I can't remember!"

Cynthia was smiling at Luca's distress, and leaned closer. "I put you in bed, gave you a big goodnight kiss, and you wrapped your arms around me and..."

"And *what*?" cried Luca.

Cynthia continued slowly, relishing Luca's discomfort. "And you said goodnight... and called me by some other woman's name."

"Really?" said Luca. "And then what?"

"Well, I certainly wasn't going to stick around after *that!*" Cynthia responded. "So, I just made sure you were tucked in tight and I went home. Your honor is still intact."

Luca breathed a sigh of relief. "Well, I am glad to know we didn't do anything stupid," he said as he stuffed his mouth with quiche.

"Would it have been so stupid?" asked Cynthia taking a sip of coffee. "You like me, don't you?"

"Cynthia," replied Luca, "we hardly know each other. You're great and certainly a wonderful dancer, but seriously, we need to take our time. Why don't you come to the game tonight, and we can go to dinner afterward and start over. We can't let loneliness be a substitute for building a good foundation. I have half a season left here, and you aren't going anywhere soon, so we have all the time we need to do this right. Agreed?"

"My, you are such an old-fashioned guy," replied Cynthia. "What are you, some kind of Galahad or something?"

"Actually," Luca said with a grin, "I prefer Lancelot, because he had a lot of flaws. I relate to him better. By the way, you never told me what name I called you by as you were putting me to bed. Do you remember?"

"I sure do," replied Cynthia. "A girl doesn't forget something like that! It's burned in my memory."

"Well, what was it?" asked Luca.

"It was a very strange name, one I've never heard before," said Cynthia. "It was something like Sammi Jo."

Luca spit out his coffee. "Sammi Jo?"

"Yes," replied Cynthia, "If I understood you correctly, you said, 'Goodnight, Sammi Jo'. Who is she, Luca? Is she your girlfriend? Wife? Best friend's girlfriend?"

"No," Luca said, "none of those! She is just a girl I was friends with in North Carolina when I played for the Durham Bulls. She helped me with my batting, and we used to go to dinner after the games. I helped her with her poetry. She's eighteen years old, for goodness' sake. Definitely *not* my girlfriend."

"Well, she obviously means something to you," Cynthia remarked, leaning closer to him and pointing her fork at him from across the table, "because a man doesn't call out another girl's name while he's being kissed if she means nothing to him."

"Yeah, well, she does mean something to me," replied Luca looking, down at his food. "We're good friends, and I really care about her, but not in a romantic way. It was sort of like an older brother and younger sister type relationship. She's really sweet."

"And a great kisser I suspect," said Cynthia, leaning back and taking another sip of coffee. "After all, you called me by her name, and I have to tell you, I gave you quite a kiss."

"I wouldn't know," replied Luca looking down as he stirred his coffee. "We've never kissed. Can we change the subject please? Are you coming to the game tonight or not?"

"Maybe," Cynthia hedged, pushing back from the table and gathering her purse. "I will need to check my schedule. What time is the game?"

"It starts at 7:05 pm," replied Luca. "I'll leave a ticket for you at the will-call window. By the way, I'll be the guy on the bench wearing number five, picking splinters out of his butt."

Cynthia leaned over and kissed Luca lightly on the lips, then teased, "And thank you, Cynthia, for taking such good care of me last night, and bringing me such a nutritious breakfast this morning to help with my hangover." Then she grabbed her keys off of the counter. "Don't forget to pick your car up at the pub, they tow them if you leave them there too long." With that, she breezed out the door with a final wave in Luca's general direction.

Luca sat there in the silence, feeling like he had just endured the most intense interrogation of his life and had barely survived. Sitting there finishing his coffee, he thought, why did I say Sammi Jo's name last night? She must have been on my mind. Then he remembered, I was going to call her to tell her about the game-winning home run!

He started to go to the phone when he remembered what Cynthia said about the car at the pub and decided that he' better do that first. Man, what a night; I am never doing that again, he thought as he searched for his car keys. Now, where would Cynthia have put them?

He found them on his dresser in front of a picture of him, Sammi Jo, and Casey, and his heart sank. Things are getting complicated, he thought as he pulled on his shirt and headed out the door.

CHAPTER TWENTY-FIVE

———————◇———————

Luca arrived at the ballpark three hours early, as was his habit. He liked to have time to relax and get his mind right before every game. Many times, he would spend an hour writing. It engaged his mind on a creative level, helped him to physically relax, and was his way of balancing the physical effort he would be facing the rest of the day. He had called Sammi Jo when he returned from picking up his car from the pub, but no one answered. Maybe he would try again after the game.

He thought about all that happened last night and this morning and shook his head. Things were happening so fast. Trying to capture it all in a poem, he made some notes and an outline but couldn't come up with an appropriate theme or arc. It was all disjointed and confused, but he knew there was an underlying cohesiveness there that he couldn't put his finger on. Maybe it had to do with new beginnings or life changes, or maybe it was about the evils of alcohol. His thoughts were all over the place.

He put his pen down and remembered that often time's hindsight provided the proper perspective. He decided to leave it alone for a few days until the impact of the past twenty-four hours became clearer.

As he was dressing for the game and preparing for his

pre-game stretching exercises, the head coach called him into his office.

"Come in and close the door, Luca," said manager Sonny Jackson. "I wanted to speak with you after last night's game."

"Sure," replied Luca, closing the door and taking a seat.

"Luca, I have a problem," Jackson started, "I have a starting shortstop that can't hit, or at least can't hit yet. I have another shortstop who can hit but is sitting the bench because the top brass has invested so much money in the non-hitting shortstop and insist that he play until he starts hitting. Understand?"

"Yes, sir, I do understand," replied Luca.

"I also have a second baseman who can't hit his weight but is a golden glove level infielder. If I take him out, I lose his defense, but his bat is killing me, especially when the shortstop isn't hitting. I can't afford to have two dead spots in the lineup like that. Are you still with me?"

"Yes, I believe I am, sir," replied Luca.

"Here is my hypothetical question," said Jackson, looking Luca in the eye. "Is my bench-sitting shortstop, who can hit, capable of playing second base well enough to give me both good defense and a good bat?"

Luca, surprised by the "hypothetical" question addressed to him, quietly thought about the answer. He had played second base for a number of games back in college.

It was sophomore year and the team's starting scholarship second baseman, his friend Tommy Hank, hurt his ankle in a pickup basketball game. It had been the opportunity that showed Coach Shane that even though Luca was only a walk-on, that he could both hit and field at the college level. It had been his big break. Tommy had worked with Luca on the techniques for turning the double play from second base, and even though it was very different from turning two from shortstop, Luca had mastered it with Tommy's help. He was sure he could do it again.

Luca answered Jackson's "hypothetical" question. "I'm sure that any shortstop who has made it to this level must have enough experience to be able to field ground balls well enough to give you what you need," replied Luca. "But I think the important part that you have to evaluate is, can he turn the double play from that side of the bag? Why don't you watch him during infield practice and make your decision then?"

"Good idea. Just what I was thinking, that would be key." Jackson stood from his chair, then looked at Luca and said, "So why are you just sitting here? Get out there and get some infield practice at second base, I'll be out shortly."

"Yes, sir!" Luca replied, jumping out of his chair. He was out the door in seconds.

Manager Jackson saw what he needed to see during infield practice, and when the game started, Luca's name was penciled into the starting lineup. He was playing second base and hitting seventh. Luca couldn't believe it, his first start at the AA level.

As he warmed up before the game started, he scanned the stands for Cynthia. The seats he had tickets for were still empty. Sammi Jo would never have been late for a game, thought Luca as he ran out onto the field to take his position, still scanning the crowd for Cynthia. Once he finished his pre-inning ground balls, he stopped worrying about Cynthia and focused on the game. His mind was going through the checklist of things Tommy had told him he had to remember when playing second. Cover first on the bunt, move up and towards second on double play situations, and get to the bag really early on double-play ground balls to the left side of the infield.

The game started and everything around him went silent. He was in the zone once again and it felt great. He was on the field, and he was at home and at peace.

"Great game tonight," said Manager Jackson to Luca after the game was over. "I think, hypothetically speaking, that I may have found a solution to my second base problem. What do you think, Luca?"

"I can't say," he replied, "but I'm sure that whoever that solution is, he is probably so happy to be playing that he will give you everything he has, guaranteed."

"That's good to hear," Jackson responded, slapping Luca on the back. "As long as he keeps hitting, I am going to stick with my solution. Maybe it'll get us into the playoffs this year and make me look like a very smart manager. Who knows?"

Luca got changed quickly and headed out to his car. He was so excited by his sudden change in fortune that he didn't even remember his tentative date with Cynthia. When he got to his car, Cynthia was standing there, hands on hips.

"Did you forget all about me?" she asked. "I kept waving to you from the stands, but you never even looked my way"

"Sorry, Cynthia," said Luca, "but when I'm in the game, I'm so focused I can't think about anything else. When did you get to the park?"

"I don't know, sometime after 8:30," Cynthia replied. "I had to finish up some reports at work and then give a coworker a ride home. Did I miss anything important?"

"Not much," replied Luca as he opened the door of his car for her, "just the beginning of the next chapter of my career. Any ideas about where you would like to go to dinner?"

Cynthia picked a place back at the waterfront that had a live band and upscale bar food. There was no wait, so they were seated right away.

"The music is awfully loud," said Luca as he held her chair for her to sit. "Maybe we should have gone somewhere quieter so we could actually have a conversation."

"I like it here," she replied. "It helps me forget the nonsense of the day."

"How can you hear yourself think in here?" asked Luca, taking his seat. "I need quiet to process the day."

"Not me," replied Cynthia. "Once the day is over, I forget about it and like to have fun."

They ordered and after the waiter left, Cynthia grabbed his hand. "Let's dance!"

"I'm pretty beat," replied Luca. "I just played nine innings, and it's late. Can I take a raincheck?"

Cynthia pouted. "Come on, I have been cooped up in my office all day, and I want to cut loose. Come on, humor me. After all, I did bring you breakfast this morning."

As tired as he was, Luca agreed. "Just a couple of dances until our dinner comes, and that's it. Agreed?"

"We'll see," replied Cynthia, leading him onto the dance floor.

As they made their way through the crowd Luca thought, what have I gotten myself into?

After dropping Cynthia off to pick up her car at the ballpark and saying goodnight, Luca couldn't help reviewing the evening in his head. He was not happy, since he had a double header tomorrow and had really just wanted to get into bed early and get some rest.

Instead, here he was heading home at one in the morning, after a night of dancing and yelling at the top of his lungs to have a conversation over the blaring music, which was still ringing in his ears. This was definitely not the way to start the next phase of his career.

Worse than that was the fact that he hadn't had any time to review the game or his performance mentally. That was something that was critical to him. It helped him identify the mistakes he had made and needed to work on the following day.

It was something that he had gotten so used to with Sammi Jo. She was always so interested, and since she was so focused on his performance during the games, she helped him work through it all and usually pointed out something he missed.

Instead, he'd spent the evening helping Cynthia work through her office issues with coworkers and bosses. It was all petty office politics stuff, and it made his brain hurt. When he got home, he got undressed, not even bothering to brush his teeth, and his last thought as he fell into bed was, I really need to talk with Sammi Jo tomorrow.

At seven a.m., Luca was awakened by knocking on his door. Looking at the clock, he thought to himself, Seriously? Who in the world would be knocking at this hour? I need at least three more hours of sleep.

He threw on a pair of jeans and headed to the door. "Hold on, I'm coming," he called, obviously annoyed. As he threw the door open, ready to blast whoever it was, he saw Cynthia standing there, loaded down with a bag of goodies once again.

"My, you are a bear this morning," she remarked as she swept by him. "I just thought that since you enjoyed our breakfast date yesterday, you might appreciate another."

Luca stared and scratched his head. "Normally, I might, but we had such a late night last night, and I have to be at the ballpark early today for a double header, so I was really hoping to sleep until ten. I'm pretty beat."

Cynthia smiled and gave him a good morning peck on the cheek. "Smells like someone didn't brush their teeth this morning. Why don't you do that while I get breakfast ready? I have to leave by eight so I can get to work on time. Please?"

Luca, knowing that she was not going to leave and let him go back to sleep, reluctantly complied once again, thinking, man, what have I gotten myself into?

The first game of the double header was a disaster for Luca. He was sluggish and had a hard time concentrating. His swing was slow, and he struck out twice. He got to the bag late on two double play opportunities, causing him to take a very hard hit from the runner on one of them. The result was a swollen ankle, which he needed to ignore. The sore ankle prevented him from stealing second at a critical point in the game and may have caused the team to lose an opportunity to tie the game in the late innings. By the time the second game started, he felt better and did reasonably well, but not his best.

After the game, Manager Jackson came up to him in the locker room and said, "Hypothetically speaking, I was not all that impressed with the solution to my second base problem today. I am hoping that tomorrow might be different. Can I count on it, or do I have to go back to the drawing board?"

"Hypothetically speaking," Luca answered, "I believe you can count on it. I have a feeling tomorrow will be better."

"It had better be," replied Jackson as he left Luca sitting at his locker, "or, hypothetically speaking, I may have to make a quick change."

CHAPTER TWENTY-SIX

Cynthia had not attended the double header, and Luca was thankful for that. All he wanted to do was go home, take a hot shower, and get into bed with his notebook. He had a few days of notes to make and review and was determined to stay awake until he had finished it all. He also needed to make that long overdue call to Sammi Jo.

Since Luca arrived in Savannah, they had regularly stayed in contact with at least two letters and one call a month. That seemed to work for both of them, and it had kept them up to date on important activities and developments. Of course, if there was anything really significant happening in one of their lives, they would call the other immediately. That is what Luca felt bad about, and he needed to correct that right away.

When he got home, he showered, dressed for bed, and picked up the phone to call Sammi Jo. Before he could dial there was a knock on the door. Luca hung up the phone and answered the door. Once again, it was Cynthia.

"Hi, Luca!" Cynthia said, pushing past Luca into the apartment. "Want to go out dancing again tonight? A bunch of people from work are going, and I would love to have you meet them."

Luca closed the door. "Not really, Cynthia," he replied.

"I'm beat, and I need to get some rest."

Cynthia pouted. "But I really want you to meet these people I work with. Please? I promise it won't be too late tonight."

"Not tonight, sorry," replied Luca. "Last night really caused me problems in the games today. I felt like crap, and I can't afford for that to happen again. Can you understand that?"

She approached Luca with a pout plastered on her face. "If you don't come, then I'll have to find someone else to dance with. You don't want to make me do that, do you?"

"Look, Cynthia," replied Luca, stepping back, "we really don't know each other all that well, and if you want to dance with someone else, go right ahead. We have no claims on each other. Seriously, I am not into manipulation and don't appreciate your approach. I need some sleep. It's important for my job to be fully rested. If you can't understand that, then I think it is best if we part as friends. Go and have a good time with your coworkers."

Cynthia looked crestfallen. "I'm sorry, Luca, I didn't mean to offend you, and I wasn't trying to manipulate you. I just enjoy being with you, that's all. Haven't you had a good time these past few days?"

"I have," replied Luca, "but it's all moving way too fast for me. Until I met you, my mind was completely on baseball, and that was working for me. I need focus and time by myself, that's the way I'm built. Now, if you will excuse me, I would like to make a phone call and then go to sleep."

"When can I see you again?" asked Cynthia.

"I don't know," he replied. "We leave tomorrow for a road trip for a few days. I'll call you when I get back, and maybe we can have dinner if I don't have a game the next day. Will that work?"

"Sure," she replied as she stormed toward the door. "Call me when you get back. I'll be around, I don't have any road trips." She slammed the door as she left.

Luca stood there looking at the closed door and thought to himself sardonically, well, that went well.

Calming himself after his encounter with Hurricane Cynthia, he once again picked up the phone and called Sammi Jo. Henry answered.

"Hey Henry, it's Luca, how's everything in beautiful Wake Forest?"

"Couldn't be better!" replied Henry. "After all, when you live in North Carolina, what could be bad?"

They both chuckled and Luca said, "I'm sorry to be calling so late, but I just finished a double header and wanted to chat with Sammi Jo, is she around?"

"Sure, she just got in a little while ago from a movie date with Bobby, and I doubt she's in bed yet. Let me get her for you, hold on."

As Luca held on, waiting for Sammi Jo to pick up, he wondered, when did Sammi Jo start seeing Bobby again? I thought that was over and done with. Before he could finish his thought, Sammi Jo came on the line.

"Hi, Luca! So glad to finally hear from you. You know we can't get any news about your team up here and it kills me, because I need to know what is going on. I thought you forgot about me"

"Never, slugger," replied Luca, "but I've had a hard time finding time to call this week. A lot has happened, and I wanted to share some good news with you; but first, I need to know, when did you start seeing Bobby again? Your dad said you went on a movie date tonight, so I'm wondering how things are going. I thought you two weren't seeing each other anymore."

"Oh, that," said Sammi Jo. "That started up again

around graduation. We had gotten back on good terms after he found out he got into Winston-Salem State University and they're willing to look at him for their football program. They told him if he makes the team, they would consider offering him a partial scholarship. It changed his whole outlook, and he wanted to make up and start over. So, we've been dating again for a couple of months."

"That's interesting," replied Luca. "How's it going?"

"Okay," Sammi Jo said, "but it's not like before. He's nice, but I'm not feeling it so much. You know what I mean?"

"I do," Luca answered. "Been there, done that, for sure. Are you working?"

"Yes, I'm back at the daycare center for the summer," said Sammi Jo. "It's fun, and the kids are great, but it's not much of a challenge. I can't wait to start at NC State in the fall, it's all I can think about. Thanks so much for setting up that meeting with Coach Esposito, he's such a legend, and he was so nice. He helped me figure out my courses and even said that I could be the team manager! I'll get to keep all the stats and help him with the travel schedule and arrangements. He really likes you, Luca. He said to tell you that if you ever want to quit baseball, he has a coaching position for you anytime you want it."

Luca laughed. "Well, he's going to have to wait a long time, kiddo. I plan on having a very long major league career. Maybe after my Hall of Fame induction ceremony, I'll take him up on his offer."

"Speaking of the Hall of Fame, how is the season going?" asked Sammi Jo. "Have you played in many games yet?"

"That's what I wanted to tell you," replied Luca. "Guess what, I just started my first game two days ago! I'm now the starting second baseman."

"Wow!" Sammi Jo exclaimed, genuinely excited for him. "But why second base? How did that happen and why didn't you call me right after the game?"

"It's a long story," Luca replied, and he filled her in on the details.

When he finished, she asked again, "So why didn't you call me right away? I thought that's what we do."

Luca was quiet for a moment, then said, "The guys took me out to celebrate the walk off homerun and then it got too late to call. The next couple of days were crazy, too. This is my first real opportunity to share the good news. I hope you're not upset."

"No," said Sammi Jo, "I understand. I'm just sad that I couldn't celebrate with you when it happened. So, you're starting every day now?"

"It looks like it," said Luca, "as long as I keep hitting and play decent in the field, I think the job is mine to lose. How great is that?"

"That's wonderful," replied Sammi Jo. "What's your schedule like for the next week or so?"

"We head down to Jacksonville tomorrow to play the Suns for a three-game series, then we'll be back here against the Birmingham Barons for a weekend series. We have a double header on Saturday and a single game on Sunday. The season is a little over halfway done, and we really need to start playing better than .500 or we'll miss the playoffs. I'm hoping I can help."

"I know you will," encouraged Sammi Jo. "You're so good, and getting regular playing time will help. I know that not playing regularly messes with your head."

"That and not getting enough sleep," replied Luca. "That's been a little hard lately."

"Really?" replied Sammi Jo, "Why is that? Been out

partying with the team?"

"Something like that," Luca hedged. "But I think I've got that under control now, so things will get better. Have you still been writing? I haven't gotten any new poems from you in a while."

"Not so much," replied Sammi Jo. "Ever since you left, I haven't been all that motivated. I don't seem to have all that much that's interesting enough to write about."

"Well, keep at it. Don't give up on it, you have a real talent. I framed 'The Cold is Coming' and have it hung up in my living room. That was a truly impressive poem, so heartfelt and bleak. It tore my heart out to think you might have felt those things. Hopefully, the sun is coming out for you, Sammi Jo. You have a bright future, and the world is yours, if you just take it. Remember that."

"I will," replied Sammi Jo. "I'll try to write something this week. How about you? Have you been writing?"

Luca laughed wryly. "Not so much, slugger, I seem to have the same problem you do. I can't find the hook. I can't take all the jumbled thoughts and find a coherent focus. Right now, all I have is a bunch of disjointed notes. I'm taking some time off from writing to see if time will provide any context. Maybe on the bus rides it will come together for me, who knows?"

"Well, my advice is to take your own advice and just write something; anything," said Sammi Jo. "You can always throw it away if it's no good, but it may start the thought process. I know you, you need to get that stuff out of your head or it'll make you crazy."

"You are so right," replied Luca, "I can feel that happening already. Hey, I have to go and get some sleep. Tell your parents I said hello, give Casey a hug from me, and I'll talk with you when I get back from Jacksonville. I have a feeling things are moving in the right direction."

"Okay, Luca," said Sammi Jo. "Have a great series and stay healthy, okay?"

"Will do, slugger. Goodnight, and I'll talk with you soon."

After hanging up the phone, Sammi Jo went immediately to Henry, who was sitting in the living room. "Daddy, I have a question," she said.

"Sure, sweetie, what's up?" asked Henry.

"Are you up for a road trip next weekend?" said Sammi Jo with a twinkle in her eye.

Luca had a very good series against the Jacksonville Suns. He hit in every game, had a few key RBIs, and played a solid defense. Feeling pretty good about himself, he drove home from the stadium thinking that he might just be on his way to the majors. He could see it in his head; just finish the season strong, help the team get into the playoffs, and get the attention of the Atlanta Braves scouts.

He might have to have another season here in Savannah, but after that, he was sure that the next stop was AAA. Even better, maybe the Braves might invite him to spring training to get a closer look at him. If that happened, then anything was possible. He was excited about the weekend series with the Birmingham Barons, his confidence was high, and he was back in his rhythm. Nothing could throw him off balance now, he thought as he walked up the steps to his one-bedroom apartment.

Opening the door while he was loaded down with his travel bag, his foot slipped on a note lying on the floor. He put his bag down and grabbed the note. When he opened it, his heart sank. It was from Cynthia.

Luca,

I hope you had a great road trip. I will see you this weekend at the games. I am sorry I was such a pain, and I promise I won't be as pushy anymore. It's just my nature to go after what I want, and right now, that's you. I think you're great. and I think we could be so good together. Please give me a second chance.

Cynthia

Cynthia, he thought. I haven't thought about her for days. I guess I'm going to have to see how the weekend goes and then fish or cut bait. This is not what I need right now.

He put the note on the kitchen table and headed into the bedroom to put his clothes away and take a well-deserved shower. Afterward, he wrote in his notebook, then before he retired for the evening, he went back to the kitchen for a glass of water.

On his way through the living room, his eyes fell on the framed poem by Sammi Jo. He stopped and read it again, thinking about how powerful it was and realized that it captured the sense of dread he was suddenly feeling. He wasn't sure why he was feeling that way after such a good series, but still, it welled up in him. Something was coming, he was sure of it.

CHAPTER TWENTY-SEVEN

"Thank you so much, Daddy!" said Sammi Jo as she and Henry approached the ticket booth at Grayson Stadium for the Saturday double header. "Isn't this great? I love these old ballparks, and it's so much bigger than where the Bulls play."

Henry chuckled. "Sammi Jo, it only holds around four thousand people, so it's not that much bigger than El Toro Park. But yes, I love the atmosphere and the sense of history."

The ride from North Carolina had taken about five and a half hours. They left at nine a.m. and arrived directly at the stadium around two-thirty p.m. This meant that they would miss an inning or two of the game, but since it was a double header, Sammi Jo was okay with that. She had slept for most of the ride, so she was full of restless energy.

"Do you think we should go to the will-call booth to see if he's left tickets?" wondered Sammi Jo.

"Why would he have left tickets for us if he didn't know we were coming?" Henry asked with a grin.

"You're probably right," replied Sammi Jo. "I'm just so used to doing that. I guess it is silly. Let's just try anyway."

While Henry kept their place in line, Sammi Jo ran up to the will-call booth and asked breathlessly, "Did Luca

Milano leave any tickets here today for the game?"

The man at the booth checked and said, "Yes, he left one, but it's already been picked up. I guess you're out of luck, sweetie."

Sammi Jo was confused but thanked the man and went back to join Henry in line. "He said that Luca had left a ticket, but someone already picked it up. Maybe he has a friend from out of town that is here today to see him play."

"I suppose so," replied Henry. "I'm sure Luca has lots of friends who would love to watch him play. Let's just get the best seats we can, and maybe we can visit with him between games. Remember, Sammi Jo, this trip is about encouraging Luca and showing him our support, it is not about us. We don't want to distract him or do anything to ruin his focus."

"I know, Daddy," Sammi Jo said. "It's just that I haven't seen him in almost a year, and I can't wait. I know this is a very critical time for him. He has to prove he can handle the starting position and do it every day consistently. I'll be as quiet as a church mouse, I promise."

Henry looked at her skeptically as he handed the money to the ticket booth cashier. "Don't make promises you can't keep, Sammi Jo. Just don't make a spectacle of yourself and that will be enough."

"Will do, Daddy!" Sammi Jo agreed as she grabbed her ticket from his hand and led him quickly toward the entrance gate.

She stopped when she got there, admiring the ancient brick of the stadium and the beautiful arches that ran around the perimeter of the main stands.

"Are you coming, Sammi Jo?" Henry called, waiting to hand his ticket to the attendant.

"Yes, Daddy," she replied, and ran to catch up with him.

They handed their tickets to the attendant, entered, and found their seats along the first base line. They were bleacher-style seats that were separated from the main stands behind home plate by a walkway leading to the field.

"They're great seats, Daddy," said Sammi Jo as she settled in with her program and popcorn and searched the field for Luca.

The first inning and a half was over, and the Braves were at bat. Luca had said that he was batting seventh, so there was a good chance they still might catch his first at bat. She strained her neck to see past the people standing in the aisle and saw Luca climbing out of the dugout into the on-deck circle.

"Daddy, I see him!" exclaimed Sammi Jo. "He's on deck, he's up next!"

She wanted to run right down to the field level seats near the on-deck circle and tell him that they were there to see him play, but she knew that would be a distraction. So instead, she took a deep breath and sent up a prayer that Luca would do well.

The first batter drew a walk, and Luca stepped up to bat. He checked the signs from the third base coach and dug in. The runner took off from first on a steal, and Luca stroked a single between second and first right behind the runner, who then advanced easily to third base.

Sammi Jo was on her feet screaming. "Daddy, did you see that! A perfectly executed hit and run!"

"Yes, honey, I saw it," replied Henry. "Now sit down and relax, we have a long day ahead of us." Sammi Jo sat down and marked the play on her scorecard and put a huge circle around it with an arrow to the margin where she wrote, *First AA hit that I saw Luca get. YAY!*

The game progressed, and the Braves were ahead by one run in the top of the ninth. The Barons had runners on first and third with two outs. A single would tie the game. With another game to play, the Braves just wanted to close this one out without having to go into extra innings so they wouldn't have to deplete their bullpen.

Sammi Jo watched Luca closely as he looked toward the catcher to pick up the sign indicating what pitch he was calling for. He looked away, covered his face with his glove, and signaled to the shortstop. Sammi Jo knew he was saying that he would cover second on the steal since the batter was right-handed. She then saw him move closer in and toward second base.

The pitch was thrown, and the batter hit a screaming one hopper up the middle. Luca raced to his right, dove, and speared the ball backhanded about ten feet behind the second base bag. Still lying on his stomach, he flipped the ball right from his glove toward second base before the shortstop was even there. The ball hung there in space for what seemed like minutes to Sammi Jo as she held her breath.

The shortstop, racing to the bag, caught the ball backhanded and stepped on the bag fractions of a second before the runner arrived. The umpire gave an emphatic out signal and the stadium burst into cheers.

Sammi Jo leaped to her feet, spilling her popcorn all over Henry. "Daddy! Did you see that play? It was amazing! That may be the best play I have ever seen Luca make. He saved the win!"

She watched as the other Braves players surrounded Luca, slapping him on the back and rubbing his head as they headed to the dugout.

"Daddy, please can I go down there now to congratulate him? Please?" begged Sammi Jo.

"Okay, sweetie, the game is over, so I'm sure there will be no harm in talking to him now. Go ahead. I'll join you as soon as I get out from under all of the popcorn you spilled on me."

Sammi Jo took off before he was finished speaking and made her way down to the seats behind the dugout. She squeezed her way past the other cheering fans and those that were heading out of their seats toward the concession stands. Luca was still standing in front of the dugout being congratulated by his coaches and teammates when Sammi Jo made it to the front row.

"Luca!" she shouted trying to get his attention. "*Luca!*" she yelled again, waving her hands and jumping up and down.

Hearing his name called, Luca looked into the stands and saw Sammi Jo. A huge smile broke out on his deeply tanned face, and he motioned for her to meet him at the side of the dugout. Extracting himself from his teammates, he went toward the gate between the bleachers and the main stands. When she got there, he was waiting for her, and she rushed to him, leaped at him, and hugged him tight.

"That was *amazing!*" she exclaimed. "That was the most incredible play I have ever seen!"

"Thanks, slugger!" Luca responded, putting her back on her feet. "What in the world are you doing here? Is your dad with you?"

"Yes," said Sammi Jo, still giddy with excitement. "We drove down this morning to surprise you!"

"Well, you certainly have accomplished that!" Luca replied. "When did you decide to do that?"

"Right after we spoke the other night," said Sammi Jo. "I had nothing going on this weekend, and Daddy said that it sounded like fun. We haven't been to a game all summer, and I really missed it."

Then Luca stepped back and cocked his head. "Let me

get a good look at you. It's been so long since I last saw you."

He looked her up and down, and Sammi Jo wondered if he recognized how much older she looked. She was dressed in blue jeans and a nice, white, golf-style shirt with white converse sneakers. Her strawberry blond hair was in a loose ponytail, but she wondered if she still looked like the young girl he remembered.

From the look on his face, Sammi Jo had her answer. His expression said he thought she was now blossoming into a beautiful young woman.

"You look great," was all he said. "Definitely a sight for sore eyes."

"And you have kept up your workouts I can see," Sammi Jo remarked, feeling his bicep. "Very impressive!"

"*Ahem*!" said a voice from the stands. "Luca, would you introduce me to your little friend?"

Sammi Jo looked up and saw a woman glaring at Luca from the front row. Luca's smile dropped a smidgen, then he put his arm around Sammi Jo and led her over to the stands to introduce her. Sammi Jo tensed up considerably as they approached.

"Sammi Jo, this is Cynthia. Cynthia, this is Sammi Jo," Luca said by way of introduction. "Cynthia, this is the girl from Wake Forest I told you about. You know, the friend that I share poetry and hitting tips with."

"Oh, yes," replied Cynthia, putting on an obviously fake smile. "The tomboy who likes baseball, I remember. You are so cute! Did your mommy and daddy come with you today?"

Sammi Jo was now bright red with embarrassment, realizing that this must be the person who Luca left the ticket for.

"My dad and I drove down today to watch Luca play.

He's like part of the family, and we wanted him to know we still care about him." Then, feeling her anger grow, blurted out, "And what's your story? Why are you here? How do you know Luca?"

"She's also a friend," Luca answered quickly, looking at Cynthia.

Cynthia looked back at Luca and then Sammi Jo. "Yes, I am a friend also, but one who has taught Luca a lot about dancing. You must know how much he has to learn in that area since you know him so well."

Sammi Jo looked stricken but recovered quickly. "No, I don't," she answered quietly. "We never talked about dancing, just baseball and poetry."

Henry had been watching from a distance, but as the awkward situation developed, he hurried to Sammi Jo's side, which she was grateful for.

"Luca!" he shouted as he approached. "So good to see you, son. What a game, what a play! So glad we could be here to see it." Then he slapped Luca on the back, turned to Sammi Jo, and said, "Why don't we let Luca get to the locker room so he can rest before the second game starts?"

"Okay, Daddy," Sammi Jo replied, glad to have her dad by her side.

"I'll see you after the game," said Luca. "We have a lot to catch up on."

Sammi Jo manufactured a smile and replied, "Sure, have a great second game."

She grabbed her father's arm, walked back out through the gate, and up the ramp toward the concession stands.

Luca looked at Cynthia. "That was cruel," he said. "Why couldn't you just have been nice?"

"Why couldn't you have told me that she was going to be here and have prepared me?" replied Cynthia.

"I had no idea; they didn't tell me they were coming. It

was a surprise," said Luca.

"Well, it looks like everyone got a little surprise today, doesn't it?" said Cynthia as she turned and stalked back up the stands to her seat.

Luca just shook his head, completely frustrated, and headed to the locker room to prepare for the next game. As he sat in front of his locker, he thought, now I know where that feeling of dread was coming from. I need to fix this quickly.

CHAPTER TWENTY-EIGHT

———◇———

"Daddy, I think this was a very bad idea; I think we should leave," said Sammi Jo as Henry handed her a drink from the concession stand.

Henry could see that she was still shaking from the confrontation with Cynthia and replied, "We can do that honey, if that's what you really want. You know that I've gotten hotel reservations for us so tonight you could go to dinner with Luca, and we planned to see some of tomorrow's game, but if you want to go now, we can do that. All I'll say is that things might not be as they seem, maybe you are jumping to conclusions."

"I don't think so," Sammi Jo responded morosely. "You didn't hear her say that she's been teaching him to dance and called me a tomboy. She implied that was how Luca referred to me. I was so embarrassed. I think they're dating, and he never even told me."

"Sometimes things like that can be one sided," said Henry. "If Luca didn't tell you about it, maybe he doesn't think that they are dating. You should give him a chance to explain."

"Oh, my goodness! He's probably going to dinner with her tonight!" exclaimed Sammi Jo. "I didn't even think about that. Daddy, I really think we should leave. I feel so stupid." She put her head on her father's chest and started to sob.

Henry put his arms around her. "Here is what I think we should do. Let's stay until after the game and give Luca a chance to make his own decision. If he is going to dinner with that other girl, then we go back to the hotel, have a nice dinner, and leave in the morning." Then he held her out from him and said, "Sammi Jo, look at me." She looked at him and he continued. "Remember, the game is never over until the last strike. Let's wait until all the pitches have been thrown before you head to the locker room. Okay?"

Sammi Jo wiped her eyes. "Okay, Daddy, if you say so."

They headed back to their seats just as the umpire yelled, "Play ball."

Luca hustled out to his position and readied himself for the first pitch. His mind was in turmoil. He hated drama and lived his life to avoid it as much as humanly possible. But now he was in a situation where no matter what he did, someone was going to get their feelings hurt. On the one hand was Cynthia, whom he liked but still had reservations about. On the other hand was Sammi Jo, whom he really cared about and felt very protective of.

He knew that if it came down to it, he would rather hurt Cynthia, but then he would have to deal with her for the next few months since neither she nor him was going anywhere. He knew he didn't need that kind of stress while he was trying to claw his way out of the minors. He needed peace of mind to be able to focus on his job.

Before he realized it, the batter hit a hard ground ball to his left. Because he was distracted, he got a late jump and it sneaked by him into the outfield for a single.

As he took the throw from the right fielder and got the ball back to the pitcher, he admonished himself. Enough! Forget the drama and focus on the game! He refocused, and from that point on put both Cynthia and Sammi Jo out of his mind. He would deal with all of that after the game.

Luca had a lukewarm game at bat with one single, a walk, and two weak grounders to the infield. The team lost by five runs, and overall, he would say that his performance was lackluster. He did his job but didn't shine; definitely not what he needed.

He hustled to the locker room after the game, took a quick shower, and steeled himself for whatever confrontation awaited him when he exited the safety of the stadium. Reluctantly, he walked out of the tunnel to where he saw Cynthia, Sammi Jo, and Henry waiting.

Taking a deep breath, he addressed them all. "Well, that was certainly a game I would like to forget. Sorry you all had to endure it."

Sammi Jo came bounding up. "I thought you played fine. After all, if you take the day on the whole, you had a very good doubleheader. Just focus on that."

Cynthia also approached him. "I may not know much about baseball, but I thought you did well. You just need to unwind a bit; you look very on edge to me. Where should we go for a nice relaxing dinner?"

Luca looked at Sammi Jo and then Henry. "What are your plans for dinner? Are you staying overnight or driving back?"

"I have reservations for us to stay the night in Savannah," Henry responded. "We planned to get up early, go to church, and then see some of the town before the game. We probably won't stay for the whole game, but we wanted to see you play as much as possible. If you already have plans for dinner, we can just see you before the game tomorrow."

"I'm sure that Cynthia wouldn't mind if you both joined us for dinner," Luca suggested, looking at Cynthia for a response.

"I'm sorry, Luca," Cynthia answered shortly, obviously seething, "but I just remembered that I had committed to a coworker to help her with a project she's working on. Maybe some other time," she said to Henry. "But I would like to speak with you before I go, Luca."

Luca knew what was coming and said to Henry and Sammi Jo, "Why don't you guys go to the hotel, get changed and meet me at The Boar's Head Grill & Tavern on North Lincoln Street in an hour? I'll speak with Cynthia and then drop off my things at my apartment first."

"Sounds like a plan," Henry responded. Then, turning to Cynthia, "It was very nice to meet you, Miss Cynthia, I hope you don't have too much trouble helping your friend. It is a very generous thing to do. Not many people would give up their Saturday night for something like that."

Cynthia forced a smile and said, "I'll try."

Sammi Jo and Henry headed toward the truck while Luca and Cynthia waited until they were out of earshot to talk.

"I can't believe you did that!" Cynthia chided. "You know I wanted some alone time with you since you've been on the road for almost a week. Couldn't you have just met them for breakfast or something tomorrow?"

"Come on, Cynthia," replied Luca. "They drove five and a half hours to see me play and sat through a double header. The right thing to do is to spend some time with them. After all, they're like family to me. I invited you, too, but you seem to have other plans."

"Do you really expect me to go to dinner with the girl who has a high school crush on you?" Cynthia asked. "I would rather stick needles in my eyes than to subject myself to that."

"She doesn't have a crush on me, we're just friends," replied Luca. "She's very sweet, and you could learn a few things from her about being nice to people."

"You are so blind," replied Cynthia, turning away. "She is so smitten with you, and I'm telling you that there is more between the two of you than you even realize. You need to wake up and understand that you should distance yourself, or she is going to get really hurt."

"You are blowing this way out of proportion, Cynthia," Luca said. "She's a sweet girl, and we share some interests; there is nothing romantic at all. She's seven years younger than me, for goodness' sake, just barely out of high school and very innocent. Just stop with the jealous nonsense and grow up. I'm going to dinner with them, and then we can finish this tomorrow, if you want. I need to get going."

Cynthia silently seethed with anger and thought to herself as she watched Luca walking to his car, she may be seven years younger, but she doesn't look it. Luca, you are so blind and walking into more trouble than you know. You need me, but you just can't see it yet.

But you will.

CHAPTER TWENTY-NINE

———◇———

Luca got to the restaurant and scanned the room for Henry and Sammi Jo. Not seeing them, he spoke with the hostess and got a table. She seated him at a table set for four and asked him if he wanted a drink while he waited. "I'll just have water with lemon, please," was his response as the waitress placed the menus on the table and retreated to fill his order.

Luca checked the door once again and watched as Sammi Jo entered and began looking for him. He stood and waved her over. Seeing him, her face broke into a radiant smile and she quickly weaved her way to the table where Luca waited, holding her chair for her.

"Thank you, Luca," she said as she took her seat. "I never get tired of this."

"Is Henry parking the truck?" asked Luca.

"No," replied Sammi Jo. "He said he was feeling tired from the long day and was going to just rest and watch some TV. He dropped me off so that we could still have our time together."

"I understand," replied Luca. "It is a long drive from Wake Forest, and then add a double header in the Savannah heat, and I can completely understand. I'm glad that we have this time together. There are so many things to catch up on."

The waitress brought Luca's drink, took Sammi Jo's drink order, and left.

"I know," replied Sammi Jo, "it's been a while, and even though we've written each other and talked on the phone, it isn't the same. Why don't you start? I really want to know the inside scoop on AA baseball, and if you don't mind, also about Cynthia. I got a weird feeling from her."

Wanting some time to collect his thoughts, Luca suggested that they decide on their order first. When the waitress returned with Sammi Jo's drink, they ordered.

When she was gone, Luca began. "Cynthia is a girl I met a few weeks back when I was having dinner alone after a game. She came up and introduced herself, took a seat, and we had dinner together. Her company transferred her here, and she didn't know anyone, so she was looking to make friends. The next night after my walk off homerun, she found me when I was out celebrating with the team. Since then, we've seen each other a couple of times. That's about it."

"Really?" said Sammi Jo. "It seems like more than that to me. She seemed pretty territorial when we were talking between games. Sounds like you've told her about me. Her tomboy remark was a little below the belt. Is she always so snarky?"

"I don't know her all that well, and she can be kind of hot and cold," replied Luca. "I can't figure her out yet, and I'm not really sure I want to make the effort. She's pretty forward, and I'm not all that comfortable with that. Think about Savannah, for example. She was so sweet, gentle, and laid back. That's one of the big reasons I liked her. She had a soft Southern charm, and I'm not looking to get into a relationship with someone who's so assertive."

"Does assertive scare you?" Sammi Jo teased with a

smile.

"No, assertive doesn't scare me," Luca replied in the same tone, then turned serious again. "It just makes me put my guard up, especially at first. I find it hard to relax when I'm with someone like that. I feel like I'm being herded or manipulated and it puts me on edge, and I don't enjoy that."

"Are you relaxed now?" asked Sammi Jo, leaning back in her chair a bit and taking a sip of her sweet tea.

Luca smiled. "Of course, Sammi Jo, why wouldn't I be? Now, enough of Cynthia, tell me how things are going for you this summer. Tell me more about your meeting with Coach Esposito, your plans for NC State, your writing, and what's going on with Bobby."

"I will, but first, I want to show you a picture of Casey! He has grown so much." She handed him a picture. "He's really great, I can't believe how much I love him. It's hard to remember when he wasn't around, you know what I mean? He has such a gentle disposition and is so smart!"

"Wow!" Luca exclaimed. "How many baseballs does he have in his mouth in this picture?"

"Three!" replied Sammi Jo. "Can you believe it? I remember when he was so small, he couldn't even get one in there. Now look at him."

"It's amazing how he has grown in such a short time," Luca observed, handing the picture back to her.

"It's been almost a year, Luca," Sammi Jo reminded him. "I guess puppies do a lot of growing up in a year."

Luca looked at Sammi Jo, noticing once again her pretty green eyes with just the right touch of makeup, took a deep breath, and replied, "Yes, they do, Sammi Jo. They certainly do."

While waiting for their dinner, they talked about how Sammi Jo was so excited to start college in the fall and how nervous she was. She was the first in her family to go to college and had no one who could give her perspective on what to expect. Luca filled her in on his college experience and how he dealt with being away from home for the first time. How being on the baseball team really helped with the transition, because he felt like he had a ready-made group of friends. He suggested that she try out for the girls' softball team in the fall to see if she could make the transition.

As much as she liked baseball, Sammi Jo had never played softball and always thought that it was silly. The big ball and the underhand pitching were things she could not handle. Plus, if she was going to be the manager for the men's baseball team, she might not have the time to do it. Luca agreed but encouraged her to look into it anyway. Their dinner came, and they continued the conversation.

"So, how about Bobby?" asked Luca. "Last time we talked, you said he was going to Winston-Salem State. He must be happy about that."

"He is," replied Sammi Jo, "but everything has gotten weird again."

"Explain that to me," Luca requested. "What do you mean by weird?"

"You would think that he would be getting excited about it, you know, the adventure of it all, and start preparing and stuff, but he has gotten really clingy lately," Sammi Jo answered. "He doesn't see his friends as much as he used to, and he wants to spend most of his free time with me. I guess I should be flattered, but I kind of like my alone time, and he gets almost pouty when I have something else to do. I don't know what's going on with him."

"Maybe he's scared," replied Luca. "Bobby was a big deal in high school, and he's probably gotten used to that.

Maybe the thought of going to a much bigger school where nobody knows him, and he has to start all over is intimidating him? Plus, he may be worried about embarrassing himself on the football field. After all, he is going to be trying out for a college team."

"I guess it could be that," replied Sammi Jo. "That kind of makes sense. But why cling onto me? I can't help him with that."

"He's trying to hold on to the familiar," observed Luca. "The comfortable relationship that makes him feel safe. You make him feel good about himself. That's one of your best qualities, Sammi Jo. You make people feel good about themselves. I can attest to that. Just understand what he is going through so you can deal with him for now. Soon, he'll be off to college, and I'm sure at that point, things will start to get better for him. Are you planning on dating him while he is at school?"

"I don't know," Sammi Jo replied with a shrug. "He's not the same as he was before, and it kind of freaks me out. Sometimes I feel like he is suffocating me. I really need to spread my wings. I don't think I want to be saddled with a relationship while I'm trying to deal with adapting to college and building new friendships and all."

"I understand and agree," replied Luca. "If you're not one hundred percent committed, it will never work anyway. You have a tough road ahead of you, and I don't envy you. You really should tell him all of this now. The longer you wait, the harder it'll be. Give him time to deal with it before he heads off to college so he can acclimate himself to the change. It's the kindest thing to do."

"Sounds like good advice," said Sammi Jo. "Maybe even good enough for you to take yourself."

Luca smiled. "Maybe so. When did you get so smart?"

"I've had a year to learn and grow," Sammi Jo replied.

"I guess me and Casey have a lot in common."

Once again looking deeply into her bright and beautiful green eyes, Luca found himself nodding in agreement. "Yes, you do, Sammi Jo, and I think it's great. You really have grown so much. I can even see that coming through in some of your writing, although you haven't sent much recently. Have you gotten past your writer's block?"

"Not really," Sammi Jo said, shaking her head. "My mind is so jumbled with all the changes coming that I can't focus well on it. Any suggestions?"

"Well, I'm kind of in the same position right now," Luca admitted. "But I can tell you that in the past, when I've had a hard time writing, I try to break out of the pattern by writing something different than I have ever written before. Most of the time, it's by trying to write something humorous or ridiculous. So much of my writing is serious or reflective, trying to make sense out of things. I find that sometimes writing about something frivolous, fun, or nonsensical can help open the floodgates. What do you think? Want to give it a try?"

"I'm not a comical person," responded Sammi Jo. "I'm not sure I could do that, but maybe I'll try. Any other suggestions?"

"Yes, you could try writing observationally," suggested Luca. "My professor in college said that when we become focused on ourselves and our own feelings, sometimes we become closed off to the world around us. Try writing about someone else or something you observed or that you remember someone else doing. Write as an outside observer of someone else or even yourself. Tell someone else's story or your own story from an outside perspective and see if that helps."

"I think I can do that," said Sammi Jo thoughtfully. "Can you send me an example so I can see how that works?"

"Sure," said Luca. "When I get back to my apartment, I'll look through my old stuff and send you some."

"Thanks, Luca," replied Sammi Jo. "I'm really looking forward to getting back into the groove. I miss it!"

They talked more about baseball and Luca's experiences in AA ball and how much better it was than single A. He told her that if he could continue to earn the starting position that he might get a shot at AAA next year, but that it was a long shot. They agreed that consistency, dedication, and focus was something they were both going to need in the next year to keep moving forward toward their dreams. They committed to keep each other on track and to tell each other when they thought they were off course.

"It's getting late," said Luca at last. "Your dad is probably wondering where you are. We'd better get going."

"I'm sure he's sleeping in front of the TV by now, he really was pretty beat," said Sammi Jo, not really wanting to leave. "I know he doesn't mind how late I stay out knowing I'm with you. Remember, I'm eighteen now, and I have been out later than this a lot of times. Can we go for a walk along the riverfront? I don't know if I'll ever be back here, and I heard it's beautiful. Do you mind?"

"Sure, that sounds great," said Luca. "Let me pay the bill, then we can walk to the riverfront from here. My car is parked in that direction anyway."

Luca called the waitress over, paid the bill, and he and Sammi Jo headed out the door toward the waterfront.

CHAPTER THIRTY

———◇———

As they approached the riverfront, the wind picked up a bit, so Luca removed his sport coat and placed it around Sammi Jo's pretty, tanned, and freckled bare shoulders. She had worn a simple sundress and was feeling a little chilly.

"Thanks, Luca, that helps," said Sammi Jo, thankful for the gesture.

As they walked, Sammi Jo was struggling a bit in her heels.

Luca looked down at her shoes, then said, "You'd better hold my hand. These streets are all made of cobblestone from here on and can be very challenging. I don't want to bring you back to your father with a sprained ankle."

Sammi Jo reached out and took his waiting hand. When she touched him, she felt an electric thrill shoot through her that took her breath away. As they walked holding hands, she could smell his cologne wafting up from the sport coat around her shoulders, and she was intoxicated by it.

Struggling to gain her composure, she asked, "Why are these streets paved with cobblestones? It's very pretty, but they are so hard to walk on."

"These are two-hundred-year-old cobblestones that

came from Europe," Luca replied. "Ships would come here for goods to take back with them for sale. But when they sailed over, they were empty, so they used the cobblestones for ballast during the trip. When they arrived here, they off-loaded all the cobblestone ballast they didn't need for the return trip because of the weight of the goods they were loading. There were so many of them from the ships that were continually coming here that the people started to use them to pave the streets. It really adds to the charm of the city, don't you think?"

Sammi Jo didn't comprehend a word he was saying, because she was so enthralled by the fact that she was walking with him, holding hands in this enchanting setting. She managed to reply, "How nice."

Luca continued, "This area was all old, rundown cotton factories until a few years ago when the city decided to revitalize the riverfront. They just finished the work a couple of years ago, and since then, it's become one of the most visited areas in the state. Beautiful, isn't it?"

"Absolutely beautiful," Sammi Jo replied, looking up at him.

As they walked the softly lit cobblestone street, Sammi Jo was fascinated by the huge churning and clanking of the cargo ships sliding along the river. They walked along, stopping every now and then to peer into the shop windows and look at the artwork in some of the galleries. Luca bought them ice cream cones, and they stopped to enjoy them on a park bench where a string quartet was entertaining the passersby.

"This is so amazing," said Sammi Jo. "Thank you so much for taking me here. It's more beautiful than I could have imagined."

"It is great," agreed Luca, listening to the music.

Sammi Jo noticed that his foot was tapping along to the

beat and said, "So, you've been taking dancing lessons from Cynthia. What has she taught you?"

"I have *not* been taking dancing lessons from her," Luca replied, slightly disgusted. "I already know how to dance. I just don't know all the most recent ones, so she thinks I need to learn. I prefer the more classic dances that I learned in grade school. The nuns at my Catholic school made us learn the foxtrot and the waltz and stuff like that, and I guess it stuck. Not much call for that type of dancing these days."

"What type of music is this band playing?" asked Sammi Jo.

Luca listened for a minute and said, "I believe it's a southern waltz. I can pick up the one-two-three, one-two-three, one-two-three timing. Watch the people dancing and notice how they move. See it? One-two-three, one-two-three. It's pretty easy."

"Will you teach me?" asked Sammi Jo, suddenly excited.

"Really?" replied Luca. "You want to learn this? Now?"

"Absolutely," Sammi Jo insisted, taking off his sport coat, grabbing his hand, and pulling him off the bench, "It'll be fun! Come on."

She dragged him to where the others were dancing and stood there. "Okay, now what?" she asked.

Luca stepped closer, put his right hand gently on the small of her back and took her right hand in his left. He said, "We have to keep our frame. That means that our arms stay at this angle and there is always about two inches between us at all times. Follow me and remember the one-two-three, one-two-three count."

Sammi Jo was trying to listen, but the blood was pounding so hard in her ears that it was hard to hear. Being this close to him and touching him like this made her knees

175

weak. A dizzying wave of warmth sizzled over her as if she had just gotten too close to a roaring fire. She struggled to focus as he began to lead her to the music. For a while, she struggled to match his movements, but after a bit, she started to fall in step with the rhythm. Luca was making it easier because he was leading so well.

"You're really good at this, Luca. Those nuns taught you well," she said.

"The most effective teaching I ever had," replied Luca. "They always carried rulers and used them to great effect. It is amazing what some corporal punishment will do to help you remember. You are doing pretty well yourself. You picked this up rather quickly."

"I'm a quick learner," replied Sammi Jo, "when I have a great teacher."

The song ended too quickly for Sammi Jo, and she stood there holding Luca's hand praying for another waltz.

The band looked like they might be finishing, so Luca said, "Stay here for a minute," and then walked up to the band leader. He handed him something, and they talked for a minute. Luca came back and said to Sammi Jo. "They're going to play a couple more waltzes just for us. I couldn't have your first lesson cut short."

Sammi Jo hugged him. "Thank you, Luca, you just read my mind!"

The band began to play, and Sammi Jo and Luca danced there along the riverfront under a perfectly full moon until long after the music stopped. Sammi Jo felt like Guinevere in the arms of Lancelot.

Eventually, they gathered their things and walked slowly back to the car, once again with Luca holding her hand to steady her on the damp cobblestone streets. Enjoying the beautiful night and the scenery, they walked in silence, each filled with their own thoughts about the evening.

"I think I'm going to try to write a poem about tonight," said Sammi Jo, breaking the silence as Luca held the car door open for her. "There was so much beauty and so many interesting things to see. I want to remember all of it."

"That sounds like a great idea. Maybe it'll break your writer's block," he replied.

"I think it just might do the trick," Sammi Jo responded. She was still shaking from the adrenaline rush and the excitement of dancing with Luca. When Luca got into the car, he noticed that she was shivering. "Are you cold?" he asked. "I can turn off the air conditioning if you want."

"No, I'm fine," she said. "Just tired. I guess maybe the four glasses of sweet tea I had with dinner are making me jittery along with the sugar from the ice cream. I'll be fine," she reassured him, pulling his coat around her tighter and inhaling the scent of his cologne. "I just need to get some sleep."

As they drove to her hotel, Luca said, "This was really great, Sammi Jo. Thanks for taking the trip down here. It was fantastic, and I truly needed it. I can't tell you the last time I've felt so relaxed and grounded. This was fun. We even got to waltz together. How great is that?"

"I know," said Sammi Jo. "It was wonderful to learn that from you. You are a man of many talents. I knew you had good footwork on the field, but I never thought you would be that good on the dance floor."

"It's all about the partner, Sammi Jo," replied Luca, "remember that. Some partners make you struggle, and some drag you down to their level. When you find the right partner, the dance—any dance—is easy."

They arrived at the hotel and Luca got out to open her

door. She exited and handed him back his coat. "Luca, this was an amazing night. Thank you."

"It was my pleasure, partner," he said, leaning forward to give her a soft kiss on the cheek. "Now, go get some sleep and say your prayers that I have a good game tomorrow. I need it after that second game today."

"I will," Sammi Jo promised, still reeling from his unexpected peck on the cheek. "I will do a *lot* of praying tonight, believe me."

"Good," replied Luca, getting into the driver's seat. "And tell your dad thanks for letting us do this. I really enjoyed it. I owe him big time."

As he drove away, Sammi Jo just stood there and watched him. She didn't really feel like going to bed. She was so energized by the evening and all that happened, but she was confused. She needed to talk to someone about it but had no one who would understand. As she was heading back inside, she decided to think about it tomorrow.

Tonight, she was just going to enjoy the feeling and burn it into her memory so she would always have it to remember.

CHAPTER THIRTY-ONE

———◇———

Luca watched Sammi Jo in his rearview mirror standing there as he drove away. He was definitely confused. He'd just had a wonderful evening and was filled with emotions that surprised and puzzled him. He had always felt protective of Sammi Jo and appreciative of their relationship, but tonight was somehow different. Really different. As he ran through the evening in his head, the main images that came to mind, that stuck out from all the rest, were her beautiful bright green eyes and the feelings he had when dancing with her.

Everything, from the dinner conversation to holding her hand while looking in the shops, dancing with her and even walking in silence felt so right. It felt relaxing and comfortable. It felt like home, and that startled him. Maybe that was why he'd kissed her, lingering by her cheek to take in the surprisingly delicious sent of her perfume.

He knew Sammi Jo was seven years younger than him, but when he was with her, that age difference didn't seem to matter. They had so much in common, and she was so engaged in their conversations that any age difference just melted away. He thought, how is that possible?

Just a year ago, he'd thought of her as a kid, and suddenly that had changed. She seems more like a friend and confidante now instead of a little sister. There's definitely a trust factor that wasn't there before, a real connection.

Putting the key into the lock of his apartment door, the thought hit him. Peace. That was what he felt with Sammi Jo, a peacefulness that was hard to describe. He could be fully himself around her. There was nothing about him that he felt he couldn't share with her or anything she would judge him for. He could be his authentic self, and that was a first.

Every other relationship he had ever had made him feel like he was not enough or that he had to improve or change in order to please the other person. That his interests and passions had to be modified or put on the back burner and were just not as important as the other person's. That he had to sacrifice important parts of himself to make the relationship work. That wasn't the case with Sammi Jo. The thought made him smile as he started to undress and prepare for bed.

As he was beginning to write in his notepad about the evening, the phone rang. Hoping that it might be Sammi Jo, he picked up.

"Hey Luca, its Cynthia. It's after midnight and I have been calling for two hours. Did you just get home?"

Luca, taking a deep breath before answering replied, "Yes, Cynthia, I just got home. Is something wrong?"

"I don't know," she said. "What could you have possibly been doing until midnight with an old man and a young girl? I would have thought you would have put them to bed around 10 p.m."

Luca could feel his frustration rising. Cynthia had a way of asking questions in such an accusing way that it made him mad. "We had dinner and then we walked along the riverfront for a while. Do you have a problem with that?"

Luca didn't feel like disclosing that it was just Sammi Jo, since he knew that would set her off.

"I see," said Cynthia, slurring her words a little. "Did they enjoy it? Did you buy Sammi Jo an ice cream cone with sprinkles, or maybe a balloon?"

By now Luca was really annoyed. "Have you been drinking, Cynthia?" not answering her sarcastic question. "You sound a little off to me. What's with the sarcasm?"

"Yes, I've had some wine, by *myself*, I might add," she replied. "I've been sitting here dwelling on the fact that you chose them over me tonight, and it hurt my feelings. I thought we had something good going, but I guess you have other priorities."

"My priority is being a good human being, Cynthia," Luca responded rather strongly. "A caring and respectful and polite human being. That means being courteous to those you care about and who care about you. They drove five and a half hours to surprise and encourage me, and I wanted to show them my appreciation. If you can't understand that, then I feel sorry for you."

"And what about me?" replied Cynthia. "Don't I deserve a little courtesy and appreciation, too? I've taken care of you and brought you breakfast and come to watch you play your ballgames. When do I get a little of that respect and politeness?"

"Seriously?" Luca asked, now really annoyed. "I'm not the one who started this. You've been driving this thing from the beginning. You haven't even given me time to breathe. Yes, you've been fun and helpful, but honestly, you're draining me. I don't have time for drama or emotional guilt trips. I have a job to do, and you're messing with my mind. I think it's better if we just end this conversation now before you make me say something we may both regret. Goodnight, Cynthia."

"Wait! Luca, don't hang up," said Cynthia tearfully. "Just tell me, seriously, do you have feelings for her? Just tell me, and I'll leave you alone. I need to know."

Luca was silent for a few moments, trying to figure out if he should just hang up or answer her question. Thoughts and images were racing through his mind as he tried to come up with an honest answer.

Finally, he said, "Truthfully, I don't know. Maybe. That's the best I can do for now. Goodnight, Cynthia." Luca hung up the phone.

He was so aggravated by the conversation that his heart was pounding, and he felt like his blood pressure was through the roof. He got out of bed, went to the kitchen for some water, and sat at the kitchen table in the dark, reviewing the conversation in his head.

As irritated as he was, he couldn't help feeling sorry for Cynthia. Maybe he had been too rough with her. All she was really doing was trying to find out where she stood with him. She was interested in him and wanted more. That wasn't so terrible, and maybe she wasn't the problem. It was just that her attitude was so presumptuous. As if they had some kind of commitment to each other already, and that brought out the worst in him. He always struggled with a quick temper, which had gotten him in trouble more times than he cared to remember. Recognizing this in himself over the years, he had developed a very stoic approach to conflict. He would just shut down and withdraw into himself to avoid reacting badly.

Recently, that had been serving him well, except for the time he decked the waiter in Durham for his disrespectful comments about Sammi Jo. Other than that one incident, he hadn't fallen off the wagon in years. Now, this situation with Cynthia was bringing it all to the surface again.

As he sat there trying to sort it all out, he reflected on

his evening with Sammi Jo and calmed down a bit. Thinking about her brought him back to a more calm and peaceful state. One where he didn't feel bad about himself. At least there's someone out there who thinks I'm great and appreciates me for who I am, that's something to hold on to, he thought as he returned to bed.

He thought about the beautiful riverfront, the peace he felt walking silently with Sammi Jo, just holding her hand. About how at home he felt. And he began to write.

There are those times of desperation
Of dark and deep despair
When the future fades away from view
And naught but fog is there

When it seems the clarity I seek,
That single sacred quest
Lies just beyond the farthest hill
Or just beyond the crest.

That's when I take my clouded mind
To where it rests at ease
And to the one that through the haze
My mind's eye clearly sees

For I behold forever
In the green eyes that I see
The cold gray fog evaporates
Life's as clear as it can be

A crystal light knifes through the night
Enveloping my soul
And lights my way to a restful place
The harbor of my home.

Cynthia had been crying, but now she was angry. She knew that it was mostly from embarrassment and humiliation and not from any actual hurt, but it was still painful. After putting herself out there, shoving aside her reservations and fear and initiating the first meeting with Luca, she had been so sure she had done the right thing. But now it seemed that she had done nothing but push him away since then. He had been so open and friendly during that first dinner that it made her want more.

And then there was the dancing, which had been fun and exciting. He seemed into it, but maybe it was just the alcohol. She poured herself another glass of wine. Where did it go wrong, she asked herself. When did he start to feel pressured? Suffocated? How had she "drained him"?

Cynthia took a slug of wine, finishing what was left in her glass. "If it weren't for that little brat from North Carolina," she said aloud, "he wouldn't be feeling this way. Just yesterday, he said they were just friends, but now when I ask if he has feelings for her, he says maybe. Why the sudden change? Something must have happened that he isn't telling me, and I want to know what it is."

She remembered that Little Miss North Carolina and her father were going to be at the game the next day, and realized what an opportunity that would be to get some details. So she poured herself what was left of the wine and began to outline her plan of attack. She wasn't going to give up so easily.

CHAPTER THIRTY-TWO

—◇—

The following morning, Sammi Jo and Henry were up early. They went to church services and then had a nice lunch at the riverfront at a little place that Sammi Jo had spotted the night before during her walk with Luca. As Henry sat quietly eating, Sammi Jo was gushing with information and details about her evening with Luca. She told him all about the dinner conversation, the cobblestone streets, the cargo barges, and the history of the riverfront. She told him about learning the waltz and everything else they did.

What she didn't tell him about were her feelings. That was something she was not ready to share. She didn't even really understand them fully herself. She also wasn't sure how her dad would take it. He thought of Luca as a nice, well-mannered, and respectful young man, maybe even as a son he'd never had. If she started talking about possible feelings toward him, that might ruin everything for all of them.

Maybe she was overthinking it? Maybe it was all just the thrill of the night, and it would all feel differently when she saw him at the ballpark today? She also thought about how Luca hadn't really behaved any differently last night and probably didn't have the same reaction she had had to the dancing and the peck on the cheek he gave her before departing. She would need time to sort this all out before ever talking to her dad or mom about it.

"What time should we leave for the park, Daddy?" asked Sammi Jo.

"We're all packed up and checked out of the hotel," said Henry, "so we can leave any time after lunch. The game doesn't start until two p.m. so we have about an hour, and the park is only ten minutes away."

"Can we leave now?" asked Sammi Jo. "I know we have to leave in the middle of the game, so I'd love to try and catch Luca before it starts, even if it's only for a minute or two."

"Sure, sweetie," said Henry, "just let me pay the bill and we can be on our way."

Sammi Jo went outside to take one last look at the riverfront. It was alive with people enjoying the beautiful summer Sunday. She tried to burn every detail of the place into her mind so she would never forget and could call it up in detail when she wanted to remember it. It had been such a magical night, and she wanted to be able to recall it perfectly. She inhaled deeply, remembering that the sense of smell was one of the most powerful ways to bring memories flooding back. She thought about the smell of Luca's cologne and reminded herself to ask him what brand it was when they talked.

Before she knew it, her dad was at her side. "Come on, honey, we need to get a move on if you're going to have any chance of speaking with Luca before the game."

Sammi Jo and Henry arrived near the end of batting practice, and Sammi Jo ran from the ticket entrance right to the gate beside the dugout without even going to their seats. "I'm going to talk to Luca," she yelled back at Henry as she ran ahead of him.

She didn't pause to watch him shake his head, knowing that she didn't have her ticket and had no idea where their seats were. Her daddy would keep track of her and find her when she finished her conversation with Luca; she wasn't worried about it.

Neither of them saw Cynthia, seated high up in the stands behind home plate, where she had positioned herself so she could get a clear view of the whole field. She smiled when she saw Sammi Jo waiting at the gate to talk with Luca.

"She's so predictable," Cynthia said to herself. "It will make all of this so easy."

"Luca!" yelled Sammi Jo, trying to get his attention before he stepped into the cage. "Luca!"

Luca saw her, waved, and then indicated he was next to bat and for her to wait there until he was finished.

Sammi Jo responded with a thumbs up sign and settled in to watch him take his swings. He looked good and was right on the ball on every swing, hitting line drives and towering fly balls off the fence. No issues with dropping the back shoulder, observed Sammi Jo to herself, sensing he was going to have a great game. When Luca finished his turn, he ran right over to her.

"Hey, slugger! See any holes in my swing?" he asked her.

"Are you kidding?" she responded. "You looked great. I love seeing you hit for power like that. The velocity of your swing has really increased."

"Yeah," replied Luca, "that's what daily workouts in the weight room will do. Wish I had realized that when I was younger. It could have made a big difference. Where's Henry?"

"I'm not sure," said Sammi Jo, looking in the bleachers for him. "He went right to the seats, and I'm not sure where they are, but I'll find him after we talk. I wanted to talk with you before the game, because we'll be leaving around the fifth inning. I wanted to thank you again for last night. I had so much fun!"

"I had fun, too, Sammi Jo, it was great to be able to spend time with you like that. It's been a long time since I felt that relaxed and comfortable."

"Me too!" replied Sammi Jo. "I think we're really good for each other." Then, catching herself, said, "You know, psychologically, I mean."

Luca smiled. "I know what you mean." He paused for a moment and took in her outfit. "By the way, I never told you how great you looked last night. You really are becoming a stunning young lady."

Sammi Jo beamed, no blushing for her today. "Really? Do you think so?" She had the same jeans on as yesterday, but today wore a very pretty blouse and cute aqua cowboy boots. She'd aimed to be more stylish than yesterday when she dressed, and it appeared she'd succeeded.

"I do," replied Luca, "and believe me, I know!"

They both laughed, then Luca said, "I have to get back to the dugout and get ready, but let's make sure to talk in the next few days. I don't want it to be so long between calls, okay? Have a safe trip back and tell your dad I said thanks."

"Sounds good to me," said Sammi Jo, smiling. "Have a great game and stay healthy."

"Will do," replied Luca as he headed into the dugout.

Sammi Jo turned to climb the stadium steps. She didn't notice Luca pause and steal a glimpse of her, a wondering look in his eyes.

Sammi Jo stopped and stood at the top of the stairs, looking out over the field. She lingered in the feeling of having been so close to Luca and reveled in his compliment. As the players started to take their positions, she headed toward the concession stand to buy some popcorn and a couple of drinks for her and her dad before trying to find him.

As Sammi Jo was standing in line at the concession stand, Cynthia came up behind her.

"Hi, Sammi Jo," Cynthia said, startling the girl a bit. "Still hungry after such a late dinner last night? It must be good to be so young."

"Hi, Cynthia," replied Sammi Jo, turning back towards the concession stand.

Smirking, Cynthia pressed on. "Luca told me all about last night when we talked after he got home. Sounds like you two had an interesting night."

Sammi Jo's face flushed with anger. First of all, she was surprised Luca had told Cynthia anything about their evening together. Second, why would he have been talking to her that late?

"Yes, we had a good time together. We always do," Sammi Jo replied sharply.

"Well, I'm sure you did," replied Cynthia. "After all, you are such good friends. He told me everything, and we laughed together about it. I guess he thinks you're pretty funny, in a cute, little sister sort of way. What did you enjoy the most about the evening?"

By this time, Sammi Jo was getting really upset. She knew she was being made fun of, and if Luca really had shared everything with Cynthia and laughed about it with her, that made everything worse.

"I guess it would have to be the dancing," Sammi Jo blurted out, looking to return the hurt. "He taught me to waltz. He even paid the band to play two special songs for us!"

"Yes, he told me about that, too," lied Cynthia, mock

pity in her eyes. "I'm surprised that you enjoyed that part of the evening, since he told me how much he struggled, trying to keep you off of his feet and in time with the music. Apparently, it was both difficult and quite funny. We laughed so hard about it that we both had tears in our eyes."

"That's not true!" Sammi Jo exploded. "Luca had a good time, and we danced really well together. He even told me how good I was, and that we made good partners!"

"Did he?" replied Cynthia. "Well, isn't he the sweetest boy! He never says anything that will hurt someone's feelings. That's one of the things I love so much about him, he is so compassionate towards people who are challenged. I'm sure he was very encouraging."

At this point, Sammi Jo was beyond humiliated and got out of line, not wanting to give Cynthia the satisfaction of seeing her cry. Cynthia was left standing there, and she watched as Sammi Jo made her way to the bleachers.

Well, that ought to do the trick, she thought. That's right, little girl, run to your daddy. I doubt you will be troubling us anymore.

CHAPTER THIRTY-THREE

Henry had lost sight of Sammi Jo, and after a time went to look for her. Running off without her ticket and not knowing where their seats were was a little impulsive, but so like her that it made him smile. That smile disappeared when he finally found her.

Sammi Jo was sitting at the base of one of the light poles with her head in her hands. She was sobbing hard enough that she seemed to have trouble breathing.

"What's wrong, Sammi Jo?" Henry asked as he crouched down beside her. "I saw you talking with Luca, and then you disappeared. Tell me what happened."

Struggling to speak clearly, Sammi Jo sobbed, "I am so stupid, Daddy! I've made a fool of myself, and I just want to go home. I'm so embarrassed."

"You're not stupid, and you're not foolish," said Henry, trying to comfort her. "Just explain to me what happened, and we'll figure it out together."

"I trusted him, Daddy, and he embarrassed me," Sammi Jo blustered out. "He told Cynthia everything about last night. Our private dinner conversation, about our dancing together, and just *everything*! They were even laughing about it together. Can you believe that, Daddy? I am so humiliated."

"Frankly, Sammi Jo, I can't believe it," said Henry. "Who told you this?"

"That horrible Cynthia told me while I was waiting in line at the concession stand," sobbed Sammi Jo. "She said that they talked about it last night after he got home. She said they laughed about how bad a dancer I was and that I was just a challenged little kid!"

"Sammi Jo," Henry said, taking her face in his hands, "you have to consider the source. Until you hear it from Luca himself, don't believe it."

"I'm never speaking to either one of them again!" exclaimed Sammi Jo. "I just want to go home and forget about Luca, Cynthia, and baseball. I want to go so far away from all of this that it can't hurt me anymore. I thought he liked me, Daddy!" she blurted out as she burst into uncontrollable sobs.

Understanding dawned on Henry's face. After a moment, he said, "I know it hurts, sweetie, but maybe you're misreading the situation and jumping to conclusions. I think you need time to sort it out, and we can't bring this to Luca now during the game. We both need to be home tomorrow, so why don't we leave now? You can rest on the way home, and then maybe things will look different tomorrow. Then, you can speak with Luca on the phone and straighten this all out, okay?"

"Yes," said Sammi Jo standing up. "Let's leave now, but I am *not* speaking to him tomorrow, or ever again."

As Henry walked silently with Sammi Jo to the car, his heart was heavy. He knew how much hurt Sammi Jo must be feeling right now, and he had no way to fix it at the moment.

He was sure that Luca wouldn't have done what Cynthia said he did, but then again, guys his age were notoriously callous. How well did he really know Luca, anyway? Just a couple of summers, really, and some telephone conversations in between. Maybe he had just been a phony all along, putting on a good show so that Henry would allow him to interact with his daughters?

As he helped Sammi Jo into the car and closed the door, he looked back at the ballpark. He heard a roar go up from the crowd and the announcer say, "That's the third homerun this year for number five, Luca Milano." He shook his head to clear his thoughts and said to himself, "No, Luca isn't a phony. Consider the source. Consider the source."

Luca was a bit tired before the game, but he'd worked up a sweat, which always helped. He'd put his head down and ran wind sprints from foul pole to foul pole in the outfield. It felt great. The physical activity was like a pressure release valve for him and getting his heart pumping and his lungs working hard was great medicine for his brain.

He had tried to keep his mind off the conversation with Cynthia last night, as he knew he couldn't afford any distractions during the game. He needed a solid performance to keep his position and helping the team to win the weekend series would go a long way towards that end. He knew Sammi Jo and Henry would be there to cheer him on, and he was hoping that maybe Cynthia would be too upset to make an appearance. He'd put those thoughts aside and ran another sprint.

After the game, Luca was feeling good. He'd had a great day at bat, did well in the field, and helped the team take the series. They were now over .500 for the first time this year and had the playoffs in sight. Things were right with the world—the baseball world, at least.

As he was dressing, his mind went to the conversation last night with Cynthia. I have to take care of that situation right away, he thought to himself, shaking off the feeling of pity he had for her last night. I don't need drama, I need peace, and no matter what, that starts tonight.

He planned to call her when he got home and end it, once and for all, and then immediately call Sammi Jo. As he walked out of the tunnel towards his car he heard, "Luca! Luca!" His heart leapt in his chest for a moment thinking it was Sammi Jo and that she had stayed to watch the whole game. He turned to see Cynthia running his way, and his heart sank.

She ran up to him and hugged him. "What a great game! I don't usually like watching, but they announced your name! When you hit that home run, everyone went crazy! It must have been so exciting for you."

Luca endured her hug for a moment then carefully extracted himself. "Yeah, it was great, but I don't really hear the crowd much during games. I kind of block it out. What are you doing here? After last night, you're the last person I thought I would see."

"Oh, that silly nonsense," said Cynthia. "I was just a little tipsy and tired. I hope you didn't take any of that seriously. Really, I don't remember much of it very clearly. You're not still upset with me, are you?"

"Well, frankly, yes, I am," Luca replied. "You were being cruel toward people I care about and said some pretty nasty things."

"I'm sure I was just a little miffed," explained Cynthia, "because you chose to go to dinner with them instead of me. That stuff passes quickly with me."

"Miffed?" repeated Luca, astonished. "Is that what you call it? Is that how you behave when you're miffed? I would hate to see what angry looks like!"

"Things like that happen in relationships, silly," Cynthia said lightly. "That's what grown-up relationships are like. We take the good with the bad. Then, we make up. Let's go to dinner and make up, okay?"

Luca immediately had a flashback. He was back in college and standing in the parking lot with Maria, hearing her lecture him that he didn't know what love was. That he had never been in a mature relationship before and didn't understand what it was like. How it took work, dedication, and commitment, and that it wasn't always fun. He shook his head to clear the thought and refocused on Cynthia.

"I've heard that crap before," he said roughly. "It's always the same. Some girl telling me that I don't know what love is, or that I don't understand mature relationships. When really all they want is an excuse to be mean or controlling or cruel and get away with it. I'm not buying it anymore.

"Have you ever read Byron? Have you ever read Donne, or Walt Whitman? No, of course not," he said, answering his own question. "If you had, then you would know what I know, that love *is* painful, but in a good way. Love does take work, but it is a labor of love. Love forgives, yes, but there has to be sorrow on both sides. That sometimes you can be in love by yourself and it still can be the most beautiful thing, because you care so much about the other person that you respect their need to be free. Believe me, Cynthia, I know what love is because I have been taught by the best. I have seen it in my head and felt it in my heart. I've written about it. I've dreamed about it. I know what I'm searching for, and it's not you. You don't even come close. So take your cruelty, condescension, and worthless, self-serving advice and sell it to some other poor guy. Just leave me alone."

When he finished, he picked up his bag and headed to his car, leaving Cynthia standing there. As he opened his car door, he heard her yelling at him, "You are so blind, Luca, you are going to regret speaking to me like that! You'll come crawling back to me when Little Miss North Carolina breaks your heart. Just wait, you'll see."

He slammed the door and sped away, feeling like a huge weight had been lifted from his shoulders. It was either that, or maybe closer to the feeling a wolf must experience when it gnaws off its own paw to get out of a trap and is finally free. Either way, it felt painfully good.

CHAPTER THIRTY-FOUR

"Just slow down, Sammi Jo," Savannah instructed her hysterical sister on the other end of the line. "Just take a deep breath and calm down. I can't understand a word you are saying."

Sammi Jo struggled to calm herself and began again. "I need to talk to you about something that I'm embarrassed to tell you about, but you're the only one who will understand," she said between shuddering breaths.

"Okay," replied Savannah. "Let me go into the bedroom, Jimmy is sleeping in the chair in the living room, and I don't want to disturb him."

Once the door was closed and she was settled on the bed, Savannah said, "Okay, tell me what you are so upset about."

Sammi Jo started to cry again but then got control of herself and began. "I made such a fool of myself with Luca." Sammi Jo went on to recount the events of the road trip. She told her about the first encounter with Cynthia, the dinner with Luca and the wonderful evening spent at the riverfront. Finally, she explained what transpired with Cynthia after that and the result. She held back describing her feelings about Luca until she assessed Savannah's reaction.

"That all sounds beautiful, Sammi Jo, except of course the interactions with Cynthia. Why are you taking it so hard? You've encountered mean girls before, and it never upset you this way. You're tough and confident and ready to give as good as you get. Why didn't you just fight back or ignore her?"

"Because," replied Sammi Jo, "this time it hurt so badly. In the past, I didn't care what anyone said. I wasn't looking for anyone's approval or friendship. I was happy with who I was and was happy the way things were. But this felt different."

"Different how?" asked Savannah.

Sammi Jo took a deep breath. "It was different because this time, I did care. I cared about what Luca thought of me, and not in just a friendly way. I really thought that we connected and became closer that evening. I felt all grown up and allowed myself to think that he might have feelings for me. To hear Cynthia say that they talked about me and laughed at me, and that Luca was just being kind and compassionate, really hurt. It humiliated me in a way I didn't think was possible. I had allowed myself to dream, and they crushed it and laughed about it."

Savannah, now having a clearer picture, said, "I understand, I've been there, sweetie, and I know it's painful. But is it possible that Cynthia was lying? Maybe she just wanted to hurt you because she likes Luca, too? She could just be jealous of your relationship with him. You need to talk with him and give him a chance to explain before you make any decisions."

"She seemed to know everything!" exclaimed Sammi Jo. "It must have happened the way she said. How could she make that stuff up? And what happens if I call him and he tells me it's all true? How could I deal with that?"

"What if he tells you that it isn't true, and that Cynthia

made it all up?" asked Savannah.

"How will I know if he's telling the truth?" Sammi Jo questioned. "I'm not sure I can trust him now. We've always been so open and honest with each other that I never had any doubts about trusting him. It never occurred to me." Then, she had a horrible thought. "Oh my goodness! What if this is payback for you breaking up with him? Maybe he's been waiting for the most painful time to hurt me and you?"

"Now you're getting crazy," replied Savannah. "You know Luca's not like that. He wouldn't do that. All he had to do was stop calling and writing, but he didn't. He obviously cares about you and the whole family. The issue is Cynthia, not Luca."

"Maybe," replied Sammi Jo, "but I can't talk to Luca. If he tells me it's all true, it will break my heart again, and I can't deal with that right now. I have to think about it for a while. Just tell me what I do right now to stop the pain. How do I stop crying?"

"I wish I knew the answer to that, Sammi Jo," replied Savannah. "Maybe just get back into your life and deal with it the best way you can day by day. You're a good writer, maybe you should write it all down and get it out on paper. Maybe when you do that, it will start to hurt less. Maybe when you read it, it won't seem so bad or will look differently to you. Some people say that helps."

"That's not a bad idea," Sammi Jo mused. "I had so many beautiful things I wanted to write about from that night, and now they seem so stupid. Maybe I should just write them all down to remind myself not to dream anymore or to not let anyone hurt me again."

"That's not what I meant," Savannah retorted. "Write about the pain, disappointment, and embarrassment. Get them out of you and onto the paper. Burn it afterward if you want, but you have to get it out of you. Not trusting and not dreaming is not a solution. Getting rid of the bad feelings will make room for the good ones to grow again, and they will. Maybe not for Luca, but for someone else."

"Do you think I'm a stupid little kid for thinking that he could ever like me? That he could feel romantically about me?" asked Sammi Jo.

Savannah laughed. "Oh, Sammi Jo! If you could only see yourself as others see you, you would never think that. You don't even realize how beautiful and strong you are. You radiate life and energy, and that's very attractive to everyone you meet. Look, I don't know what Luca's feeling, but I can tell you that any guy would be a fool not to see how great you are, and Luca is no fool. It may be the age difference that's keeping him at a distance. You're eighteen and he's twenty-four.

"I know that in the long term that's not a huge age difference, but at this point maybe it is, for Luca at least. But also, he's immersed in his career and that takes priority over everything else. Maybe he doesn't want to allow himself to think about you that way because it would all just be too hard. Do you understand?"

"I guess," replied Sammi Jo hesitantly, "but maybe it's more than that. Maybe he really thinks I'm immature and stupid, and he's just tolerating me because he doesn't want to hurt my feelings. You don't really know if that's true or not, do you, Savannah? Right now, I'm feeling really down on myself, and I don't know that I can open up to any more pain. I think I have to take a break from Luca and the whole situation, give it a few months, and then maybe I can build up the courage to face him again. But right now, I'm feeling pretty crushed."

"I can understand that," said Savannah, "but what is Luca going to think when you stop talking with him? He won't understand."

"Maybe he can ask his girlfriend, Cynthia, and they can laugh together about it," Sammi Jo replied bitterly. "Or maybe he won't even care. If he really thinks he is doing me any favors by just being nice and kind and compassionate, then maybe he should be left in the dark. Maybe when he doesn't hear from me for a while, he'll realize how great our relationship was and what he lost."

"Maybe," countered Savannah. "That could happen, but my final advice to you is to do what you believe is right. If you want to walk away, that's your choice to make. Just realize that every choice has consequences, and you have to be able to live with them. Make your decisions carefully."

"I will, Savannah," replied a worn and weary Sammi Jo, "and thanks for talking with me about this. I'm so tired, I just want to sleep forever. Tell Jimmy I said hey."

The sisters hung up and Sammi Jo crawled into bed, thinking about all her sister had told her. I have to write this all down and get it out of me, she said to herself, and got out of bed. She took out her notepad and began to write.

We make decisions every day,
We choose the path to take.
Determining the kind of world
Our decisions will create.

Decisions are the turning points
Defining who you'll be,
What's important in your life,
Your priorities.

Make your decisions carefully.
Reflect before you do.
For if you make them foolishly
Your decisions will make you.

CHAPTER THIRTY-FIVE

Luca was sitting alone in his normal seat at the back of the bus, feeling pretty good about the road trip. He hadn't done anything spectacular, but had contributed, and that was always a positive. The team had split the four-game series on the road and was still one game over .500, and that was the main thing. Thankful for the short trip back from Columbus, Georgia, he was looking forward to a long shower and a day off tomorrow. Being so tired he couldn't even write, he just closed his eyes and let his mind wander.

The first thought that came to his mind was dancing with Sammi Jo, and he smiled. I really need to call her, he thought. We never touched base after the game, and I should have called to make sure they got home okay. I guess I was just so focused on the nonsense with Cynthia that I put everything out of my mind. He resolved to call Sammi Jo the next day and then drifted off to sleep.

He was jerked awake by the sudden movement of the bus and the sound of tires squealing. Before he could react, the bus started spinning wildly, and he was thrown violently to the floor. Equipment bags, beer cans, playing cards, and magazines flew everywhere, and then everything went black.

Luca woke up alone in a hospital room. He had no idea

why he was there or what had happened to him. He found the nurse's call button and pressed it repeatedly.

After a few minutes, the nurse appeared and wrestled the call button from his hand. "That's enough of that, young man."

"What am I doing here?" Luca asked her. "What happened to me? How long have I been out?"

"Now don't go getting yourself upset," replied the matronly nurse as she straightened his sheets. "You can't let yourself get so agitated. You need to lie still and rest."

"But I need to know what happened," pleaded Luca.

"The doctor will be in shortly, and he will tell you what he thinks you need to know. Just be patient." As she left the room, she added, "And don't go mashing that call button again, I'm very busy with other patients, and you don't want to get on my bad side."

Luca lay in the bed, struggling to remember. The last thing he could recall was getting dressed after a game, but what game it was, he didn't know. It seemed like ages ago, and there was nothing he could recall before or after that. He looked down and noticed one leg was making a bigger lump under the sheets than the other, so he tore the sheet off and saw that his right leg was in a cast up to his thigh. He tried to move it and a searing pain shot through his whole body. His mind was assaulted by a vision of being tossed around and thrown to the ground, but again, he couldn't remember when or where it had happened.

He grabbed the call button again, pressing it over and over, not fearing the wrath of the matronly nurse. He needed to know what happened to him, and he wanted answers now!

"You'd better be glad that I'm here instead of Nurse Kettering," said the doctor, strolling into the room reading Luca's chart, then taking the call button from his hand.

"With all that racket you're making at the nurse's station, she might have come in here and broken your other leg."

"A broken leg?" repeated Luca. "I have a broken leg? How bad is it, doctor? When can I play again?"

"One question at a time," replied the doctor, pulling a chair closer to the bed. "I'm glad to see you awake and alert. We were pretty concerned as the days went by."

"Days!" exclaimed Luca. "How many days have I been out?"

"Three," replied the doctor. "We were worried you might be headed for a coma. Now, just relax and be quiet while I examine you."

The doctor conducted his examination, checking Luca's eyes and chest and testing reflexes. He moved Luca's leg a bit and checked the feeling in his right foot. When he was finished, he said, "Well, the rest has been good for you. Neurologically, you are doing as well as can be expected given the severe head trauma you received in the crash. The leg is healing, and since you are a young, strong athlete, it will heal well, so that is the least of my concerns. Tell me what you can remember. What is your last complete memory?"

"All I remember is getting dressed after a game, but I can't recall what game it was," replied Luca.

"Do you remember your name?" asked the doctor.

"Of course," replied Luca, suddenly aware that maybe he didn't. "I'm... I'm... not sure. I know it will come to me, just give me time." He frowned, suddenly annoyed. "Just ask another question."

"Do you know your profession?" asked the doctor.

"Yes, of course," replied Luca, "I'm a baseball player. I remember playing in a game and then getting dressed afterward, I told you that."

"Do you know what team you play for?" asked the

doctor gently.

Luca struggled to pull the name from his memory. Nothing came to mind. "No, I don't," he replied, now slurring his words a bit and finding it suddenly hard to speak clearly. "But I will, just give me time."

The doctor stood from his chair. "Yes, time is what you need, along with more rest. I don't want you struggling with this. Your brain has received a significant injury, and you need to stay calm and peaceful. I will prescribe some light sedatives for you. Do what the nurses tell you to do, and I will be back tomorrow. For now, just rest, and don't watch the TV. It will stimulate your brain too much."

After the doctor left, Luca lay there, still in the dark about what had happened to him or when he could return to his team, whatever team that was. As he strained to remember his name, his team, and what city he was in, he heard a soft intake of breath and the rustling of clothing. He turned to see who had made the noise, fearing that it might be Nurse Kettering.

There in the doorway was a very pretty blonde, blue-eyed beauty with her hand over her mouth and tears in her eyes.

"Luca, I'm so happy to see you awake and alert. How are you feeling?" she asked softly as she came to his side and kissed his forehead. He must have looked confused, because she then asked, "Do you remember me?"

Luca stared at her, trying to recall her name. "I'm sorry, but until you said my name, I didn't even know who I was. I seem to have forgotten an awful lot. How do you know me?"

"I'm your girlfriend, silly," replied the girl, smiling. "Don't tell me you don't remember this," then she kissed him gently on the mouth, lingering there and then pulling back slowly. "I'm Cynthia, and we've been dating for more than a month. I'm sure you will remember soon, but for now, tell me all that you remember, and I will help you fill in the blanks."

Cynthia listened while Luca described what he could remember. Together, they determined that the last memory Luca had was getting dressed after his last home game. He didn't remember anything after or before that. Inexplicably, Cynthia just smiled each time he said he didn't remember something.

"So, you don't remember the road trip to Columbus? Or even our discussion after your last home game?"

"No," replied Luca, "that's all gone. I suppose I might remember eventually, but for now, I've got nothing. Please tell me how I got here and what happened."

"I read about it in the Savannah Tribune," she said, grabbing his hand and leaning in closer. "The article was at the bottom of the front page, and I happened to see the headline as I passed the news stand on my way to your apartment after buying the usual breakfast goodies for us at the bakery. The article said that the Savannah Braves team bus had crashed on the way back from Columbus, Georgia.

"Apparently, the driver swerved to avoid a stalled car stuck in the middle of the road and spun out of control. The bus rolled over three times, and you were thrown out of the rear window. Thankfully, no one was killed, but half the team sustained injuries that will prevent them from playing for at least a few weeks. You are the most seriously injured. I've been here every day since then, visiting you and just praying that you would come back to me."

"Wow," replied Luca, "that's crazy. I can't remember any of that."

"I know," replied Cynthia as her eyes started to fill with tears once again. "The doctor said that you were very lucky not to have sustained more than a severe concussion and a broken leg. He was concerned that if you didn't wake up soon that you might fade into a sustained coma. I was so frightened!" She laid her head on his chest. "I thought you might never come back to me."

Luca awkwardly put his hand on her head and stroked her hair. "I'm sorry that you were so worried, and I'm sorry that I can't remember you right now, but I'm sure I will soon. Just give me some time and try to help me remember."

"I will, Luca," replied Cynthia. "I will fill in all the blanks for you, and we'll start over where we left off. Then, when you are released, I'll take care of you. You are going to be getting a lot of attention from me, mister. I don't want to lose you again."

CHAPTER THIRTY-SIX

Fall 1982

Sammi Jo had taken Savannah's advice and had been writing feverishly for weeks to get the pain and humiliation out of her, and it seemed to be helping a bit. She had also avoided anything to do with Luca or baseball. Luca had not called or written since they returned from Savannah, and she was starting to be okay with that. She wasn't prepared to talk with him and knew that she would need more time before that could happen. She focused on her work and preparing for college.

She had even taken the difficult step of breaking things off with Bobby. Even though it was one of the most difficult and uncomfortable things she had ever done, she felt better after it was over. Bobby was hurt, but he eventually seemed to understand that they both were making new starts, and it would be better if they went to college free from any old baggage. They agreed to stay friends, but Sammi Jo didn't believe it. They would surely grow apart, and their relationship would become nothing but a shared high school memory.

School would be starting in two weeks, and she was excited by the prospect of a new beginning. The last part of the summer had been so hard. She'd experienced new and disturbing aspects of life and of herself that made her long for tranquility and simplicity. She hadn't been hardened by the experience so much as she had been awakened. What she had felt for Luca was so powerful that it had changed her. It opened her eyes to what was possible for her. The experience with Cynthia had also changed her, but in what way, she wasn't yet sure. Right now, she knew that it had made her wary and more cautious when dealing with people, but what other effects it might have down the road would have to be seen.

Sammi Jo had also avoided talking with her parents too much about her feelings. She loved and respected them, but this was all so personal and embarrassing. She had let herself believe that she'd fallen in love with Luca and that he had felt the same way. How could she discuss that with them? They still thought of her as their little girl, and to admit that she had grown up feelings about a guy seven years older than her would just result in the same old advice. "It is just puppy love," or "the first time is the hardest," or "you are too young to really know what love is".

She couldn't bear to hear that stuff. She knew it was real, and no one could ever convince her otherwise. Even now, as hurt as she was and as mad as she was at Luca, she still held out hope that it had all been a mistake. That he would see Cynthia for the horrible person she was, dump her, and then show up at her door here in Wake Forest one day and apologize for being so blind.

As she lay there on her bed, she put her dreams of the future aside and began to write to get rid of the pain and to encourage herself. She knew that she was young and had her whole life ahead of her, so she tried to focus on that as she formulated the words to write. Would she allow her recent experience to change her for the worst, or would she hold on to who she knew she really was? She knew it was a choice that she could and would have to make. She wrote,

Hold on to your innocence,
Keep it safe within your heart.
Its illumination lights your way
When all around is dark.

Hold on to your innocence,
It's God's most precious gift.
Once it's lost it's gone for good
And will be sorely missed.

Don't long for the apple from the tree,
You'll have it someday soon,
Nor reach inside Pandora's Box
When you possess the moon.

You see life through the crystal eyes
Of one whose heart's still pure,
You gather the magic of the world
In hands still young, unsure.

Your innocence has a value
Far worthier than gold,
And if you keep it safe inside
You'll have treasures yet untold.

She reread what she had written and tried to believe it. Many times when she was writing, she knew that she was writing about hopes, dreams, and wishes more than reality. That was one of the things that she would always be grateful to Luca for. He had taught her to dream and had helped her see beyond her own little world. The poets that he had introduced her to had opened her mind up to a whole new world of love and beauty, hopes and dreams, heartache and passion. And, if they were destined to go their separate ways, at least she would always have the beauty and magic of poetry to remember him by.

She put her notepad aside, feeling a little better, and as she drifted off to sleep, her last thought was that she really should call Luca soon, maybe even tomorrow.

CHAPTER THIRTY-SEVEN

———◇———

"Do you need anything else, Luca?" asked Cynthia as she straightened up the kitchen of his apartment. "I have to be heading home, but if you need anything from the store, I can add it to my list and pick it up on my way back here tomorrow morning."

Luca, struggling to get changed for bed, replied, "No, Cynthia, I'm fine. You've already stocked the refrigerator, gotten all my prescriptions, and done everything but actually feed me my dinner. I think I can survive until morning."

Cynthia smiled to herself as she dried the last of the dinner plates and put them away. "I love being able to help you recover, Luca. It's a joy for me." She put the dish towel aside and walked back to the bedroom, where she found Luca exhausted in his night clothes, recovering from the effort of getting ready for bed.

"You really should let me help you with that," Cynthia chided. "You know that the doctor said you shouldn't strain yourself. It could set you back."

"We've already talked about this, Cynthia," said Luca as he raised himself to a sitting position on the bed. "I still don't remember you very well, and I don't feel comfortable letting you help me get dressed. I have to do some things for myself. Just give it time, and I'm sure I will remember. Can you be patient? Wait until my memory comes back, and then we can start over."

She leaned closer and gave him a gentle kiss on the cheek. "Of course, sweetie. I'll be patient, but don't take too long, we have a lot of catching up to do. I'll see you in the morning. Don't stay up too late, you need a good night's sleep."

"Goodnight," said Luca as he watched Cynthia head to the kitchen to get her bag and leave. Hearing the phone ring, he shouted, "Can you get that, Cynthia?"

"Sure," she replied and picked up the phone. "Hello, Luca Milano's residence, who is this please?"

Sammi Jo couldn't speak. She had summoned up the courage to reach out to Luca after all these weeks and now the first voice she heard was Cynthia's. Overcoming the shock of realizing that Cynthia was at Luca's apartment, she finally found her voice and angrily said, "It's Sammi Jo, let me speak with Luca."

"I'm sorry, I think you must have the wrong number," replied Cynthia, and quickly hung up the phone.

"Who was it?" asked Luca from the bedroom.

"Just a wrong number," she replied, smiling to herself. "I'm going to leave the phone off the hook for the rest of the night so you aren't disturbed while you are trying to sleep. I'll see you in the morning before I go to work. Rest well." She left the receiver on the counter and headed out the door.

Luca got under the covers and reflected on the past few weeks. His stay in the hospital was comfortable but mind-numbing. He enjoyed the visits from the other players and the manager as they helped to pass the time and fill him in on a lot of what he had forgotten about the season. And, of course, the visit from his parents had been great, but as always, too short. They had been so worried when the team owner called them and filled them in on the accident and his injuries. He had apologized for not calling them immediately and explained that it had taken time to find the contact information. They had gotten the first available flight to Savannah and were there the day after he had awoken.

They were so thankful to Cynthia for all of her attention to Luca while they had not been there, and they really seemed to like her. They had all gotten along well and had even gone to dinner a couple of nights to get to know each other better. It was all so bizarre to Luca. He still didn't remember anything about Cynthia, and to see her and his parents getting along so well was just weird. Especially because they had confirmed that he had never told them he was dating her.

Before they left to go back to New York, it was Luca's mom who agreed that it was a good idea that Cynthia continue to check in on him daily to make sure he was recovering well and taking all his prescriptions. Cynthia had been thrilled and agreed readily.

Sure, she was attractive, and any guy would be happy to have such a pretty and attentive girlfriend, but Luca still felt uneasy, as if something wasn't right. He felt as though he was living someone else's life. As he reached for the bottle of water that Cynthia had left on his nightstand for him, he noticed a notebook lying on the floor. It seemed very familiar, and he got a sense of comfort when he picked it up. Opening it, he started to read some of the earliest entries. Much of it was about baseball and his analysis of the games, with notes about adjustments to his swing and other hints and observations. Reading further, Luca started to hope that reading about his past might trigger memories that would help him remember more.

He read his thoughts and notes about when he started playing in Durham. He had some broken recollection of that, and it seemed familiar and comforting.

Reading more, he eventually got to an entry about a "giant hayseed" guy who was stalking and harassing him, and then about hitting a girl in the stands with a bad throw. At that point, he stopped and put the notebook down for a minute. Reading about that gave him butterflies in his stomach for some reason. He was confused and struggled to call up the memory, but nothing came.

Reading further, he read about the family he became friendly with and their daughters. He had been interested in the oldest girl, Savannah. From what he wrote he must have been quite smitten with her. Apparently, it didn't last.

At that point, Luca was mentally exhausted from the effort of reading and trying to remember, and decided to turn in. He placed the notebook on the nightstand and turned out the light. There would be plenty of time to dig into it.

I'll read more tomorrow, he thought to himself as sleep started to overtake him. I also need to remember to ask Cynthia about this. As my girlfriend, she may be able to help me put it all into context.

The next morning, Cynthia arrived bright and early, and as usual was loaded down with breakfast goodies. Luca was already up, as the pain in his leg and the intermittent headaches and nausea made sleeping for long periods of time a challenge.

He sat in the living room, fully dressed, once again trying to read through and remember the entries in his notebook. He looked up and asked Cynthia, "Have I ever mentioned the Jacksons from Wake Forest? Have we ever discussed my time with the Durham Bulls?"

Cynthia blanched. She collected herself and replied,

"Sure, they were a family you were friendly with for a while when you played there, but you haven't heard from them in ages. I think you felt sorry for them because you hit their daughter with a baseball. You haven't talked about them much, so I just assumed it wasn't very important. Why do you ask?"

"I found this notebook on the floor next to my nightstand. Apparently, I've been writing in it for years. I'm not very far along, but I'm hoping that it will help me remember. You know, trigger something in my brain that will unlock all of the stuff I've forgotten."

"Luca, you know that the doctor said you have to be very careful about overstimulating your brain!" she scolded, approaching him on the couch. "He didn't want you constantly dwelling on remembering and reading strains your eyes and your brain. He wants your recovery to progress naturally, and that can only happen if you rest your brain."

Cynthia took the notebook out of his hand and returned to the kitchen. She put the notebook down next to the receiver. It was still off the hook, and she let it stay that way. "Come sit down at the table," she said. "I have breakfast for us, and you have to take your medicine. No more talk about North Carolina or baseball or remembering. Let's just enjoy the moment, okay?"

Sammi Jo was furious that Cynthia had picked up when she had called last night and then hung up on her. She had called back at least a dozen times after rechecking the number to make sure that it was correct. Every time, the line was busy. Boy, they must be having a grand old time talking about me and laughing, she thought. How could I have been so stupid to open myself up to that kind of hurt again after coming so far in the last few weeks? Still, I would love to give both of them a piece of my mind. Today will be the start of a new day, she promised herself as she dressed for work. No more innocent, naïve Sammi Jo. I have to get tougher and stronger. I have to learn to fight for what I want and to give as good as I get.

As she walked out the door, she caught a glimpse of the phone hanging on the wall, and it made her sad. She remembered the first time Luca had asked to talk with her and how it had filled her stomach with butterflies. She put the thought out of her head and reminded herself, it's a new day, Sammi Jo, and a new you. Toughen up!

CHAPTER THIRTY-EIGHT

Spring 1986

"See y'all after the ceremony!" said Sammi Jo as she grabbed her cap and gown and bolted from the truck before it even stopped moving.

"I swear that young'un is going to give me a heart attack," complained Granny from the back seat of Henry's truck. "She moves so quickly from one emergency to the next. When will she ever slow down?"

"She just didn't want to be late for the ceremony, Mama," said Violet. "They all have special assigned places in the procession, and Sammi Jo did not want to be out of order. We will all have time to relax together this afternoon when it's all over and we're celebrating back at the house."

"Well, I hope so!" said Granny, completely flustered by all the commotion.

"Have either of you spotted Savannah and Jimmy?" asked Henry. "They were right behind me when we entered the parking lot, but now I can't see Jimmy's truck."

"Yes, there they are next to the gate," Violet answered. "They must have taken the first parking space they saw. See if you can park near them, Henry, I want to help with the young'uns."

Henry found a space half a row away and parked.

"Violet, I'll help Granny, you go ahead and help Savannah with the kids."

Sammi Jo raced to the tunnel under the stands of the Reynolds Coliseum, where her graduating class was gathering for the procession. When she found some of her fellow classmates, she said a silent prayer of thanks and stopped to catch her breath.

"Are you going to be okay?" asked her friend Marybeth.

"Yeah," said Sammi Jo, "in a minute. I just didn't want to be late, and I was afraid I wasn't going to be able to find anyone in this crowd."

"Well, you've found us now, so just take it easy!" replied Marybeth. "We have a long day ahead of us."

"I know," said Sammi Jo as she started to catch her breath. "It's just that this is such a big deal to my family, and I don't want to mess anything up. My sister and her husband even came all the way from California to see me graduate! Can you believe it? They surprised us when they arrived yesterday, and it has been such a whirlwind since then. They even brought my nephew and niece with them. I've never met either of them before. It was amazing!"

"Sounds like a lot of excitement in a short period of time," observed Marybeth.

"Yeah," replied Sammi Jo, "but all good. I am so thankful that my family is together. I haven't told anyone about the job interview I just got. But now I can do that this afternoon when everyone is together celebrating at the house. I'm really glad Savannah will be there, because I know she'll help me deal with my parents."

"Why are you worried about sharing such good news?" asked Marybeth. "Won't they all be thrilled?"

"Not when they find out the job is in Memphis, Tennessee," replied Sammi Jo. "I'm afraid Mama and Daddy will freak out. They've never even thought about me leaving home before I was married. It's kind of a thing with my family, they're kind of old fashioned that way."

"I know what you mean," replied Marybeth as she straightened Sammi Jo's cap. "My sister was the first one to leave home after she graduated from Meredith College and took a job in Charlotte. You would have thought somebody died or that she'd moved to Sodom and Gomorrah! Will it help that your sister has been in California for a few years now?"

"Maybe," replied Sammi Jo, biting her lip. "But she got married first and then moved out. I just hope that maybe they've been softened up by the experience. We'll see."

"Hey, it's nine o'clock and everyone is lining up," said Marybeth. "Get in line ahead of me. Since we're the only two women in the Sports Science degree program, we need to stick together."

"You bet," replied Sammi Jo. "Maybe I should have stuck with the classic literature degree," she joked. "There are a *lot* more women in that group. I wonder if they'll let me walk with them even if I just have a minor in classic literature."

"Don't even think about it, Samantha Jolene!" warned Marybeth. "After all we have been through together, I won't let you abandon me now. Turn around and start marching!"

Sammi Jo used the time during the boring parts of the graduation ceremony to reflect on her college experience. She'd been determined when she started at North Carolina State University, and that determination had carried her far. Marybeth had been a godsend, and they had supported each other through the trials of being the only females in a male-dominated program. More than once they'd had to stand up for themselves and prove that they were just as capable as anyone else there.

It had taken the baseball team some time to warm up to the idea of a girl giving them advice, too. After a few tongue lashings from the coach, the players begrudgingly did as she suggested, and their attitudes toward Sammi Jo improved along with their game. Soon, she was accepted fully and had a great time helping out. It was her favorite thing about college, and she was glad Luca had called the coach in her behalf.

Luca… She hadn't thought about him in a while.

"Sammi Jo, stop daydreaming!" Marybeth hissed in her ear. "We're about to go up!"

Sammi Jo shook her head to clear it and smiled as she stood up with the rest of the graduates. She was about to get that diploma, and boy, had she earned it!

"Sammi Jo!" yelled Violet. "Stop playing with Casey and come over here and blow out the candles on your graduation cake. I want to get it back inside and cut it before the flies carry it off to who knows where."

"Coming, Mama," called Sammi Jo as she threw the baseball one more time and watched Casey lope off after it. "Come on, Pat, let's go get some of Mama's carrot cake before Daddy and Jimmy destroy it."

As they went to join the rest of the family around the cake, Pat said, "I am going to miss you if you get that job in Memphis. It won't be the same around here with you gone. Then I'll have to deal with my mama and Granny all by myself."

"I know," replied Sammi Jo. "That's one of the things I'm not sure how I'll handle. I'm really going to miss you." She stopped walking, turned, and gave Pat a huge hug. "You really have been such a friend to me, especially through the tough times."

"The Luca thing?" asked Pat.

"Yeah, that," said Sammi Jo, "and a million others, too. I don't know how I would have survived without you nearby. You really helped me get my head on straight and see that I had a world of possibilities out there waiting for me. You've been a lifeline, Pat. With Savannah gone, you became my sister. I will never forget, no matter where I am."

"You know I love you, right?" asked Pat.

"Absolutely. Friends, sisters, and baseball partners forever!" replied Sammi Jo as she hugged her cousin one more time.

Her nephew, Jake, came running up and grabbed her pant leg. "Aunt Sammi, Granny says you and Pat have to come now, the flies are eating all of the cake! Hurry!"

Sammi Jo allowed herself to be dragged to the table by Jake with Casey running up behind.

When they arrived, her dad began his speech.

"Today is a great day. Not only because we have the very first college graduate in our family's history, but because today, I have seen a miracle. When God blessed us with Sammi Jo, she was the answer to Violet's and my prayers. After losing our little Silas shortly after he was born, we dared not hope that God would bless us again. But then along came Sammi Jo.

"She was an angel. She was a blessing. She was our baby girl, and we cherished her.

"Over the years, she and I became very close. We did everything together. She was always willing to try anything and always brought a sense of wonder and curiosity to whatever we did.

"As she grew, I began to feel guilty about something. I knew in my heart that she was working hard to fill the gap she believed was in my life because my only son had died shortly after he was born. She worked very hard to give me that companion I never had.

"I was not blind. I could see it. So could her mother, and as time went on, I believe that Sammi Jo recognized it, too.

"I can tell you all today that the bravest thing my daughter ever did was to put all of that behind her and grab hold of her own future. To become the woman that stands before you today. It was hard, and it was tough. She went through some very trying times, but she stands before us today a mature, grounded, well-educated, and self-confident woman. She is ready to take on the world, and to me, that is a miracle.

"It is a miracle because even though the world has tried to crush her spirit, her faith and fortitude has overcome it all. For that, I thank God.

"Sammi Jo has told us all that she may be taking a job in Memphis, if all goes well with her interview this summer. In the past, I would never have allowed that to happen. It would have been too painful for me and her mother. But today, another miracle has taken place. God has given me peace about it, and I believe assurance, that this is all in His plan for her. So, on such a miraculous day, join me in congratulating our Sammi Jo on her graduation from college and on the new, wonderful, and exciting life that awaits her!" Henry lifted his glass of sweet tea and the family did the same. "To Sammi Jo. May you find all the happiness you deserve."

Sammi Jo, stunned and uplifted by her father's beautiful speech, rushed to him and hugged him tightly. "Daddy, I never knew you knew," she said through sobs. "I just wanted you to have everything you would have had with Silas. I just wanted you to be happy."

"I know, Sammi Jo, and that says so much about you," replied Henry. "You have always made me happy, and I wouldn't have traded a minute of our adventures together for anything in the world. Now, stop crying and go help your mother cut the cake. This is a celebration!"

Sammi Jo hung on for a moment longer, gave her dad a huge kiss on the cheek, and bounded off to help Violet in the kitchen.

Henry wandered off to where Casey was sitting next to the big oak tree near the driveway and squatted down to pet him. "I am going to miss you, too, big guy. You take care of her, you hear? Make sure she keeps her feet on the ground. Okay?"

Casey just looked at Henry and rolled over to let him rub his belly.

"I guess that means you understand," Henry said, laughing. Then he gave Casey the best belly rub of his life.

Savannah came over to join her dad. "Are you going to be all right, Daddy?" she asked.

"I guess so. Do you think I am doing the right thing?" he questioned, standing up.

"I honestly don't know, Daddy," Savannah responded as they walked back to the house. "All I know is that Sammi Jo is different now."

She put her arm around her father and continued. "I think she needs this. I think she has something great waiting for her out there, and we need to let her go find it. She has always been such a searcher, analyzing everything and always doing things for others. It's time that she puts all of her energy into herself, and unless we let her go, that will never happen. We have to trust her and let her become all that she can be."

"What if she gets hurt again?" asked Henry. "I can't bear to see her go through what she went through with

225

Luca again. That was truly painful for all of us. I thought we were going to lose her."

"But she survived, didn't she, Daddy? It made her stronger and more determined to follow that dream of hers. To find her 'Camelot'. She will find it, Daddy, of that I'm sure."

Henry took Savannah's hand and nodded his head in agreement. "I guess it's my turn to be brave," he admitted. Then, they walked together to the table to get some of Violet's amazing carrot cake.

CHAPTER THIRTY-NINE

Summer 1986

"Milano!" shouted the bench coach. "Get in there and pinch hit for Stevenson, and listen, all I want is a clean sacrifice bunt. Got it?"

"Got it, coach," Luca called back, jumping up from his normal position at the end of the bench and grabbing his helmet and bat. Stretching a bit before getting into the on-deck circle, he still felt residual pain from the old broken leg. *Four years, and I still feel it,* thought Luca as he took his practice swings. It was a constant reminder of the day his life and career had changed.

He finished his on-deck routine and approached the batter's box. He checked the third base coach's signs to make sure he was still bunting, stepped into the batter's box, and dug in. *No sense telegraphing what I am going to do,* he thought as he tried to look as if he was going to swing away.

The first pitch was way outside, so he took it for a ball. Stepping out of the box, he checked the signs again and stepped back in. The next pitch was right down the middle and perfect for bunting toward third. He laid down a perfect sacrifice bunt and the runners on first and second advanced easily as he was thrown out by a wide margin at first. As he headed back to the dugout, he thought, at least I can still do that well.

He slapped the hands of his teammates as he descended the dugout steps, then put up his helmet and bat and retook his habitual position at the end of the bench. As he sat there, he thought, has it really come to this? How did I become that old utility player I used to look down on when I was a hotshot rookie? Now I'm lucky to get to pinch hit late in the game or pinch run for the slowest guy on the team. As he sat there, his thoughts went back four years to when it all started going downhill.

He was laid up for weeks after the accident, but the team still had enough healthy players to finish the 1982 season. Of course, with the low quality of the substitute players they had brought up from their single A affiliates, they finished the season well below .500 and didn't even come close to making the Southern League playoffs.

The team had been very supportive of him during his recovery and made a big deal of it when he was able to join them on the bench for the last game of the season. They had "Luca Milano Day" at the ballpark, and he threw out the first pitch, even though he was still on crutches.

After the season, he met with the coaches and management, and they assured him that he would still have a spot with them next season. They encouraged him to do his rehab work and get into top shape in the off-season. He left the meeting feeling hopeful and committed to doing the work that would get him ready to play the following year.

Of course, he wanted to head north, to spend the off-season with his family and get back into the gym where he had always done his off-season workouts, but Cynthia would have none of it.

She'd convinced him and his parents that it would be

better if he just stayed in Savannah and spent the off-season there, since that was where he was going to play next season and the continuity would be good for him. Cynthia wanted to continue to take care of him, and they had become pretty close, so everyone had agreed.

Maybe that hadn't been such a great idea; as it turned out, Cynthia was a significant distraction. In the past when he was up north, he would get up early, go for a run, come home and have a protein drink, then head to the gym, help some of the clients with their workouts, and spend the rest of the day working out. Then, he would come home, have a good home-cooked meal, and write for the rest of the evening.

Now, Cynthia would come for breakfast, bringing all sorts of unhealthy goodies, and then return for lunch. Luca didn't get out of the apartment until after noon and was pretty sluggish in his workouts by that point. He would do the work within the limits of his injuries, but the intensity was missing, and he wasn't seeing as much progress as he had hoped. He would then head home, shower and dress, and then meet Cynthia after work for dinner and, when his leg was better, dancing. She was convinced that dancing was better than weightlifting or running for his leg, and she was pretty insistent about it. He didn't have the energy to argue.

Although his leg was healing as well as could be expected, his mind was still in a fog, and he had battles with nausea and dizziness. The doctors felt that he had recovered as much of his memory as he was going to for now, and they were satisfied that he had progressed sufficiently enough to resume normal activities.

But Luca knew there was something missing. There was still so much he couldn't remember, and that really bothered him. It gnawed at him constantly. It invaded his dreams and disrupted his focus when working out. Early on, he had expressed his frustration to Cynthia, and that did not go well.

She seemed to take his focus on the past as an insult. She couldn't understand why all the "trivia of the past", as she called it, should be more important than the present. Why couldn't he just be happy with what they had and let go of what he couldn't remember? After all, if there was anything important he needed to remember, wouldn't she have told him about it? Didn't he trust her? After the first few arguments, Luca got tired of the struggle, which made his brain hurt even more, and just gave up talking about it. If his memory came back, it would have to do so in its own time.

Cynthia had also suggested that they move in together, "Just to share costs, and so she could be there to care for him every day." She had gotten really upset when Luca said no. They didn't talk for a day or so, but eventually, it blew over and things went back to normal.

By the end of the off season, Luca had gained ten pounds and had lost significant muscle mass. His leg still hurt when he ran, but he was able to push through it and had not lost more than a step or two. He convinced himself that he was in no worse shape than when he first came up as a rookie, and he would work hard during the season to get back to where he had been before the accident. That never happened.

He had lost the starting second base job to one of the new players on the team, and that set him back emotionally. He got dejected and his attitude suffered. Finally, the manager called him into a closed-door meeting to discuss it.

"Sit down, Luca," said the manager. "I need to figure out what's going on with you, and I don't want any nonsense. I want the truth."

Luca, not really surprised by the question, replied, "At the end of last season, you assured me that I would have a place on the team, and I took that to mean that the starting position was mine until I proved I couldn't handle it. That isn't the case. All I have been doing is riding the bench. How can I get back into the swing of things if I don't get any playing time?"

The manager pointed his finger at Luca and said, "First of all, we never promised you the starting job, just a spot on the team to prove you could still do it. Second, you came back here completely out of shape. I know about your struggle and the challenges, and frankly that's the only reason you're still here. From where I stand, you didn't hold up your end of the bargain."

Luca couldn't really argue that point. "Look, this has all been harder that I thought it would be. The pain hasn't gone away, and I still can't remember as much as I had hoped. My reflexes and coordination are fine, it's just my focus that has been disrupted. I know I can get that back, and I promise I will. Just be patient with me. Give me a few more at bats and let me contribute, and I know that will help get my mind back in the game. I really want to be here, and I need this. It's the one constant that I have, and the thing that makes me feel alive. Don't give up on me yet."

The manager sat back in his chair and considered what Luca had said. "I like you, Luca, and you really did well last year. If you can commit to getting back in top shape physically, I will get you more playing time. But I need to see commitment, and I need to see the fire in your eyes. Understood?"

"You got it, coach," Luca said, jumping out of his seat. From that point on, Luca laid down the law with

Cynthia. No more breakfast meetings, no afterhours dinners and dancing. It was going to be all about getting the fire back in his belly and striving to get back into top shape. He dove into his reconditioning regimen with a fury, eating right, spending every opportunity at the gym, and getting proper sleep. Still, it was significantly harder than he expected, and Cynthia was still a distraction.

Becoming sullen and withdrawn, she still managed to call or visit at various inopportune times, giving Luca significant guilt trips. He usually just listened and endured the depressing atmosphere, but even when she left, a cloud hung over him.

With the increased physical activity, he felt his mind clearing, and he was starting to have flashbacks. Bits and pieces of memories would come while he was sleeping or daydreaming, and that, too, encouraged him. He even remembered the notebook that Cynthia had taken from him months ago and decided that with his memory improving, he needed to get it back from her. He felt sure it was the key to filling in the gaps, so he decided to call her. He took a deep breath to steel himself against the expected depressing conversation and dialed.

"Cynthia, it's Luca," he said when she answered. "I have a question. What did you do with that notebook you took from me back when I got home from the hospital? I want to dive into it again to see if it will help me remember."

There was silence on the other end of the line for a while and then Cynthia replied, "I don't know, I assume it's there with you at your apartment. That was so long ago, I don't remember where I laid it down. Do you really think you should be looking at that now? It'll just depress you when you realize you can't remember any of it."

"Something in me is telling me I need to read it,

Cynthia," Luca said, deflecting her response. "Things are getting clearer, and it could be the key to unlocking all of what I have forgotten. Please check your apartment for it, and I'll look around here. If you find it, bring it with you the next time you come."

"All right, I will," replied Cynthia as she hung up the phone.

She then went to her bedroom and picked up the notebook that was on the nightstand beside her bed. There is no way you are getting this back, Luca, she thought as she opened it to read a few lines to confirm her decision. There is nothing in here that you need to remember; it will only destroy everything.

CHAPTER FORTY

———◇———

Luca was jerked back to reality by the roaring of the crowd as the final play of the game was made. His team had won, and he had contributed a great sacrifice bunt. That was as good as it got these days for him. He stood to congratulate his teammates and gather his equipment.

Not looking forward to another night alone in his apartment in Memphis, he asked a few of his teammates about their plans for the evening. A few of them were going to The Rendezvous for ribs and beer. That sounded like a safe enough event, so he decided to join them.

The Rendezvous was a uniquely Memphis joint, he noted as he descended the steps to the restaurant from the alley entrance across from the Peabody Hotel. The atmosphere was incredibly casual and aromatic, filled with the smoke and sizzling sounds of cooking meats. He and the others took seats around a table covered with a red and white checked tablecloth and ordered a round of beer and massive quantities of ribs.

Luca enjoyed being around the younger guys. They reminded him of the energy and excitement he used to feel for the game. He barely remembered the feeling. Their dreams were on the road to coming true, and they were having the ride of their lives. All they had to do was enjoy every minute of it and hang on tight. As for Luca, he still had dreams, but they felt like they were fading away, and he had to work very hard to hold onto them.

Mike Miller, the starting second baseman, handed him a beer. "Nice bunt today, Luca," he said. "It really set up the big inning."

"Thanks," Luca responded as they clinked their beer bottles together in congratulations. "I'm glad I can still contribute."

"You do more than that," replied Mike. "You're like another coach out there. When I first came here, you were the one that taught me that double play pivot move that I use every day. I'd never seen that before. Your experience and understanding of the game gives us confidence when you're out there on the field."

"Yeah," said Luca, "that's what seven years in the minors will do, give you experience, knowledge, and perspective, but not a starting job. Again, I'm glad to be of value. I actually wish I could remember where I learned that pivot move, but hey, I guess it doesn't matter now."

"Are you tired of all of this?" asked Mike. "I mean, if I thought I would be here at AA level for another four years, I don't think I could handle it. How do you do it? Why do you do it?"

Luca took a big swig of his beer and turned to face Mike. "I do it because I still love the game, and I know there will be some big payoff at the end of the road. I have no idea what that payoff will be, but I know it's coming. I can feel it."

Then, finishing his beer, he put the empty bottle down on the table. "You know about the accident I had when I was with the Savannah Braves, right?"

"Yeah," replied Mike, "everyone knows the story."

"What you don't know," Luca said, speaking a little

louder as the noise in the room elevated when a few more of the team joined them, "is that that accident took a lot of things from me besides a major league career. It took my memories, it took my self-respect, and it took my poetry, but I don't blame baseball for any of that. The game has been good to me for longer than it should have been. It has been a place of healing and of hope for me. It has been my home for a long time now, and I can't imagine my life without it."

"Wow," replied Mike, ordering them both another beer and chomping on a rib, "I never knew all of that. When did your memory come back?"

"About a year after the accident," started Luca, "I started to have flashbacks and fragments of memories started to surface. It was very confusing, and I couldn't put them into context. I had an old notebook I used to write notes in almost every day when I was playing for the Bulls in Durham. After the accident, I thought that reading through it might help me remember. Just as I started it, my ex-girlfriend took it from me under the pretense of it causing too much stress in my brain.

"Months later, when the memories started to surface, I asked her about it, and she said she didn't have it. I looked everywhere for that notebook, and it was nowhere to be found. I started to get suspicious that she must have still had it and was keeping it from me. I showed up unannounced one night at her apartment, and while she was in the kitchen, I excused myself to go to the bathroom. I looked into her bedroom, and there on her nightstand was the notebook."

"Really?" asked Mike incredulously. "Why had she kept it hidden from you? Why didn't she want you to have it if it would help you remember?"

"That was exactly the reason," replied Luca taking a big

swig of his beer. "When I confronted her with the notebook, she began to cry. She said that she was only trying to protect our relationship from what was written in the notebook. That if I read it, it would ruin everything."

"What was in the notebook that was so terrible?" asked Mike, taking another slug of beer.

"As I found out later that night when I read it cover to cover," explained Luca, "it was basically a three-year journal of my life, and it painted a picture of baseball, poetry, and love.

"It filled in all the gaps in my memory, and it clearly showed that I had broken up with Cynthia *before* the accident because of all of the cruel things she had done to people I loved, and that I was actually in love with someone else. The accident had made me forget all of that, and that is exactly what Cynthia wanted.

"After the accident, realizing that I had no memory of the breakup or of all the cruel things she had done to the girl I loved and her family, or even the poetry I used to write, she just inserted herself back into my life. Of course, she had learned from her mistakes and twisted herself into the image of a loving, doting, and solicitous girlfriend. It was all fake, all a lie, and it cost me a lot."

"What happened to the girl you were in love with?" asked Mike, now extremely interested in the story. "Did you call her when you realized all of this? Did you ever get back together with her?"

"It was complicated," replied Luca. "She was a lot younger than me and had just started college. I figured that if she hadn't called me since the last time I saw her in Savannah, she must have moved on. After all, we hadn't spoken since shortly before the accident, and more than a year had gone by. Besides that, I'm not even sure she felt the same way I did. We had never gotten to talk about it, and I had no idea if my love would be returned.

"We'd always had this kind of big brother, little sister thing going on, though that all changed for me one night in Savannah, but I never got to talk with her about it after that. Then the accident happened, the amnesia, then Cynthia, then the trade here to Memphis. Life moved on. She probably graduated from NC State this summer, and I'm sure she has big plans for her own life now and doesn't need me messing it up."

"Don't you think she would understand all of this?" asked Mike grabbing Luca's arm. "I mean, none of it is your fault. What if she felt the same way as you and would still want to have a relationship?"

Luca laughed, then took another sip of beer. "What would I have to offer a twenty-two-year-old college graduate with her whole life ahead of her?" asked Luca. "I am a twenty-eight-year-old, almost has-been minor league baseball player with a bad memory and no poetry left in my heart. That was one of the things she loved about us, we really connected deeply through poetry. It was this whole other crazy level of connectedness that was unique to us.

"I've lost that now, and I don't know if I can ever get it back. I would just be offering her an old, broken down, out-of-shape ballplayer who can't write anymore. Don't you think that would just be selfish?"

"Why don't you let her decide for herself?" came a voice from behind him.

Time slowed down. Luca felt himself slowly turning around in his seat. In those seconds before his eyes focused on the speaker, Luca felt his heart ignite in his chest and for the first time in many years, a spark of hope. Luca saw a magnificent young woman standing there with her arms crossed. He stared into her beautiful green eyes and his heart stopped. Her strawberry blonde hair hung to her shoulders and framed a stunningly beautiful, tanned face.

"Sammi Jo," he said in a whisper almost to himself, then struggled to stand and winced as the old broken leg pain returned.

She backed up a bit to make room for him. "I'm sorry to have been eavesdropping, but you guys are all so loud that a girl just can't help but overhear."

Mike replied, "Well, if that's all it takes to get a stunner like you to come to the table, then I am going to start yelling!"

Luca shot him a quick look, which made Mike go back to his beer.

"Sammi Jo," Luca said, "what are you doing here? I mean, this is crazy."

"I'm here for a job interview tomorrow for the athletic trainer's job at Overton High School. I heard that there was a game today. You know me, I can't be anywhere and not catch a little minor league baseball."

"Wow!" said Mike, still eavesdropping. "A beauty who loves baseball. Doesn't get any better than that! Pull up a chair, sweetie, and let me give you all of my inside secrets of the game."

Luca shot him another look, pleading silently with him to be quiet, but Sammi Jo stopped him. "Let me handle this," she said.

She turned to Mike. "After the game you had today," she said solemnly, "it seems to me that I'm the one who should be giving you some inside secrets about hitting." The whole table exploded into laughter, and Mike turned as red as the barbeque sauce on the ribs he'd been eating.

"Can we go somewhere else and talk?" asked Luca.

"Sure," replied Sammi Jo. "I'm staying at the Peabody Hotel across the street. It's pretty quiet there in the lobby lounge."

Luca threw some money on the table and left with Sammi Jo, his heart beating wildly out of control.

CHAPTER FORTY-ONE

◇

They found a quiet table away from the piano player and near the fountain in the middle of the room.

"Did you ever see the 'Duck March'?," asked Sammi Jo, taking her seat as Luca held her chair. "I saw it this morning after I arrived. It was so cute!"

"Yes," replied Luca. "I've been in Memphis so long that I see those ducks in my dreams."

"What else do you see in your dreams?" asked Sammi Jo.

"Besides you? Just a lot of sadness and regret," Luca replied, looking down at his calloused hands. "My dreams aren't much fun anymore."

The waitress came, and they ordered a couple of glasses of wine. When she left, Luca asked, "So, did you know that I was playing here in Memphis?"

"Actually, no," replied Sammi Jo. "As I said, I'm here for the interview tomorrow and decided to kill some time by going to the game. As you might remember, or maybe not, I love to keep score, so I bought a program. When I looked over the rosters, I saw your name and couldn't believe it. My heart started pounding, and I actually thought about leaving. But then the old memories came flooding back. The good ones. I don't know if it was because I was in the stadium, or the sights and sounds of the game, but I remembered you as you used to be, so caring, encouraging, and kind, and I sat back down. I wanted to see you again to make sure you were okay."

"How did you end up at The Rendezvous?" asked Luca.

"After the game, I came back to the hotel to change and asked the concierge for the best barbecue place in town and he sent me there. Since it was only a short walk right across the street, it was an easy choice. I couldn't believe it when I saw you walk in. You passed right by me."

"Seriously?" asked Luca.

"Seriously," repeated Sammi Jo. "It felt so strange realizing that I had become a total stranger to you. I was hurt and once again thought about leaving, but then I overheard your conversation. All of it. I'm not sure I understood it completely, but it made me want to know more. Especially about the accident."

Luca's mouth went dry at the thought of telling his story to Sammi Jo. He was thankful that the waitress had returned just then with their drinks. After she left, Luca found the courage to begin.

"That Sunday, after you and your dad left to go home to North Carolina, Cynthia was waiting for me outside the locker room. We had a terrible fight the night before on the phone, and she was the last person I thought I would see. I told her that it was over, and I never wanted to see her again. I ended it, for good.

"The next day, the team headed to Columbus, Georgia for a series against the Astros. On the way back from the series, the bus crashed and flipped over multiple times. I was thrown from the bus and sustained a broken leg and a very serious brain injury. I was out for days. When I woke up, I had lost most of my memory. Cynthia took advantage of that and portrayed herself as my current girlfriend. I really had no idea who she was, but she spent every possible minute with me helping me recover and never let on that we had broken up."

"Did she ever tell you about what she did to me at that last home game before we left?" asked Sammi Jo.

"Yes, eventually," replied Luca, "but it was more than a year after the event and only after I forced her to tell me. She had even taken the notebook that I used to write in every day and hid it from me. But after finding it in her apartment, I confronted her. I was furious. She saw how angry I was about her deception, so she confessed everything in the hopes that I would see that she had only done it because she was in love with me. It was her last-ditch effort to hold on to what she thought we had. She even told me that she had hung up on you when you called the night I got home from the hospital."

"Yeah, that really hurt," said Sammi Jo, looking down at her drink. "That really killed me. After the picture she painted of you and her laughing at me, to hear her pick up the phone in your apartment, well, I just wanted to die."

"Why didn't you call back?" asked Luca. "If I could have spoken with you, I'm sure it would have sparked my memory. It could have changed things for me, for us."

"I did call back," replied Sammi Jo, "so many times that my finger hurt, but the line was always busy. She must have taken the receiver off the hook. After that, I just gave up; I had to move on. I was sure that you wanted nothing to do with me."

"That was never true!" exclaimed Luca. "Even though I couldn't remember you, or our times together, you were always there in my heart. I knew that things were not as they should be, that there was something more important than anything else that I had forgotten. Like some dream that I couldn't recall upon waking and was constantly trying to piece together. When I finally read the notebook after getting it back from Cynthia, it opened the floodgates of my memory and broke my heart. I was a mess for weeks and everything went downhill.

"I had just started to get back into top shape and was getting more playing time and things were coming together, but after reading the notebook and realizing that so much of what I loved had been lost, it broke me."

"Why didn't you call or write me? You could have explained it all, and I might have understood," asked Sammi Jo, reaching across the table to touch his hand as he had done to her so many years ago.

"I thought about it," replied Luca, "but I had no idea if you felt about me as I felt about you. Then I thought about the age difference, and that you were just starting college, and maybe you were still with Bobby, and I didn't want to cause you more pain or confusion. Like I said, I was a mess and in no condition to make good decisions.

"As time went by, it got harder and harder. Then, I was traded here to Memphis, and I guess I just forced myself to move on. I'm sorry, I should have been braver and followed my heart. I should have trusted in you more. I can't imagine what you must have thought of me."

"I may have moved on," said Sammi Jo, "but I never wanted to, and I never stopped loving you. After that night in Savannah, my life changed forever. That evening with you was the highlight of my life. I have never before or since felt anything close to the way you made me feel.

"When you took my hand to help me walk on the cobblestones, I felt fire run up my arm and electricity shooting through every part of me, and it made me dizzy and weak. Dancing with you was heaven. Just to be able to be that close to you, smell your cologne, and feel your heart beating next to mine as you led me around the dance floor was a dream come true.

"That dream, those memories, have sustained me all these years. It is my model. It is my goal. It is my Camelot. If not with you, then with some other man. But Luca, I don't know if I can find it again with anyone else. That's the part I really struggle with. Can you understand that? Do you have any idea?"

"I do understand, Sammi Jo," replied Luca, "because it's the same for me. But I'm afraid that I'm a different person now after all I've been through. The guy you knew is gone. Back then, I was on my way to big things with a major league career on the horizon. I had poetry in my heart and dreams that were coming true. I knew who I was. I was comfortable with who I was. I was proud of who I was. That's all gone now. I haven't written anything in years, and what's worse, I don't seem to remember how. I'm going nowhere fast. All I could offer you would be a life of obscurity, so very different than what it should have and could have been."

"And what's so terrible about a life of obscurity?" asked Sammi Jo as she studied the calluses and scars on his hands. "Most of the world lives in obscurity. I live in obscurity. My parents live in obscurity. Savannah and Jimmy live in obscurity. The only thing to fear about living in obscurity is living there alone. If you have someone in your life that thinks you are the world, then you have everything.

"If you are the most important thing in the world to just one person, you are not insignificant. A small, minor league life can feel like the big leagues if you have a major league love."

She reached into her bag and pulled out a piece of yellowed paper. She unfolded it and laid it down in front of him. "Here is the poem I wrote about that night in

Savannah. It was a year or so later, and the memories were still so strong that I had to get them down on paper so I would never forget." Luca looked down and began to read.

The Secret Harbor of My Soul

A secret place of refuge
Out of time forever more
Where peace and passion mingle
Where love shines clear and pure

There lies my secret harbor
Where I send my soul to play
Among the shining memories of
One perfect summer day

Laughter lights the shadows there
Making all things new
My dreams become reality
And worries fade from view

A walk along the cobblestones
Is a gift from up above
The whispers on old sidewalk steps
A dialogue of love

These secret harbor memories
My life's most precious hours
Intoxicate my reverie
With love's most fragrant flowers

Be my secret harbor when
Life's waves crash on my shore
Be my secret harbor

so that I may become yours.

And when I am transformed into
That safe place in your heart
Then miles and years may separate
But our souls won't be apart.

Luca was in tears by the time he finished. It took him a few minutes to compose himself. "This is so beautiful," he said, looking up at Sammi Jo. "I once tried to write something similar about us and started with the same harbor metaphor. But my brain was so scrambled that I can't recall if I ever finished it. How strange is that?"

"Not so strange for two souls that have become one," replied Sammi Jo softly. "But even this poem cannot fully capture what I felt that night with you. That night, touching you while walking, my heart was so full that I felt that if you weren't holding my hand, I would have floated away into the night sky. It was the greatest feeling I have ever had."

"Funny," replied Luca, "I feel the exact opposite now. These past few years since regaining my memory, the only thing that has kept me from crashing to the ground and drowning in my misery, was the thought of you. The memory of you has been holding me up. So while you were keeping me afloat, I was keeping you from flying away," observed Luca. "That's pretty poetic, don't you think?"

Sammi Jo reached across the table and grabbed Luca's other hand. Looking deeply into his red, tired, worn, and tortured eyes, she observed, "Maybe there is hope for us yet. What would life be like if we both just let go of the things holding us down, dragging us under, and held each other's hands and floated away together?"

Looking across the table into the bright, crystal green,

tear-filled eyes he saw in his dreams every night, he replied, "It would be like hitting a walk-off home run in the seventh game of the World Series. But that doesn't happen in real life for people like us, does it, Sammi Jo? That only happens to other people. It only happens in dreams."

"Then let's dream it together," she begged. "Please? You still remember how to dream, don't you, Luca?"

Luca stood from his chair and threw a twenty on the table. "Would you like to go for a walk?" he asked, extending a shaking hand toward Sammi Jo.

"Sure," replied Sammi Jo, standing and quickly grabbing his shaking hand in both of hers. "Where?"

"I don't care," replied Luca. "Anywhere. Nowhere. Everywhere. Wherever I walk with you, Sammi Jo, will be a boulevard of dreams."

They left the Peabody Hotel, hand in hand, and began to walk the dark, dream-filled streets of Memphis. Music wafted from one of the buildings and they listened, holding onto each other for dear life.

As they got to the corner of the street, Luca suddenly stopped and extended his hand,

"May I have this dance?"

Sammi Jo gently took his hand with tears in her eyes. "You have no idea how many times I cried myself to sleep recalling the memory of the night we danced together in Savannah. I wrote about it and even wrote a happy ending, but I never thought we would ever really have the chance to do it again. Certainly not here in the streets of Memphis."

Luca, taking her hand and leading Sammi Jo in a simple waltz, replied, "Do you remember me telling you that when we put our feelings, even wishes, into words, they seem to find a way to come true? That even if life unfolds and it doesn't look exactly as you had imagined, you can work towards the dream? You can love it into being and create your own happily ever after. Do you remember, Sammi Jo?"

"I remember," she answered. "That's what kept me going on so many nights when the memories were pulling me down. Now that it really is here, I feel lighter than a feather. Hold me tight Luca, and never let me go."

He held her tighter, they kept dancing, and together they just floated away into the night.

ABOUT
THE AUTHOR

Domenic Melillo is the author of the popular Swords of Valor Trilogy, a historical fiction and fantasy adventure tale. He is also the co-author of the science fiction novel *Einstein's Desk*, on which he collaborated with his brother, renowned brain expert Dr. Robert Melillo.

A former college baseball player and longtime poet and lyricist, he has brought two of his passions together in writing his first love story, *A Major League Love*.

Originally from Uniondale, New York, he now lives in a small town in North Carolina with his wife Susan and their beloved black German shepherd Elvis on a beautiful horse farm amid stacks of physics books, poetry anthologies, historical swords, and Batman memorabilia.

CPSIA information can be obtained
at www.ICGtesting.com
Printed in the USA
LVHW101256010221
678008LV00019B/145

9 781952 103193